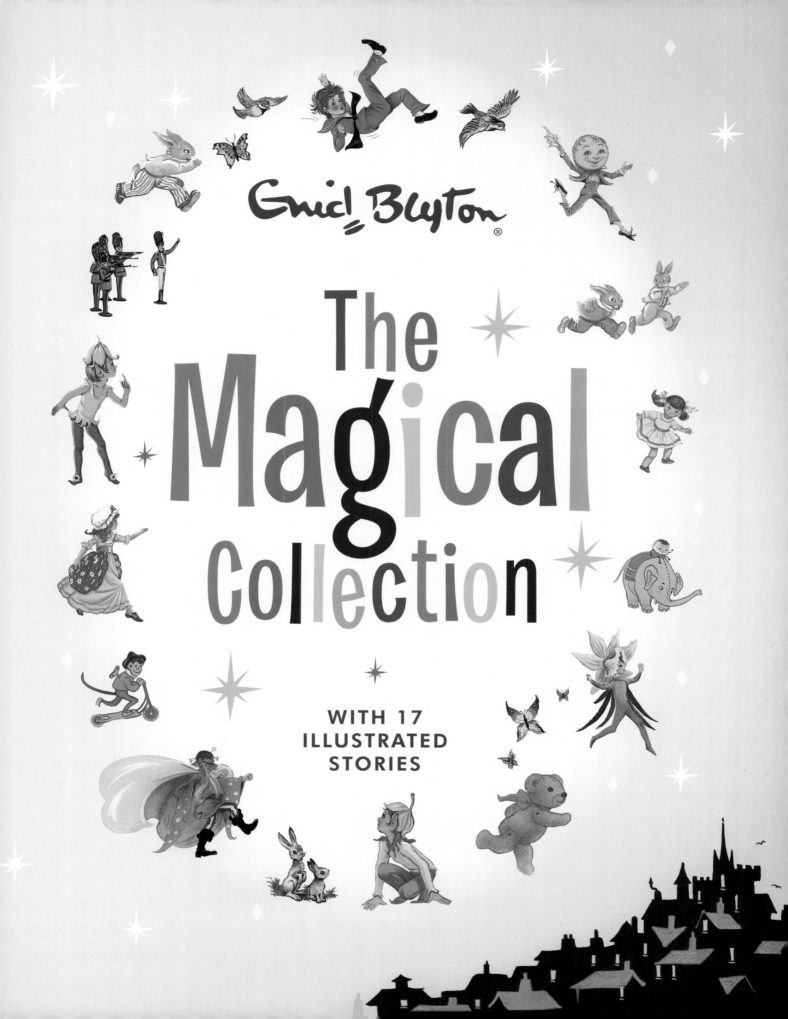

Enid Blyton

The Magical Collection

WITH 17
ILLUSTRATED
STORIES

EGMONT

We bring stories to life

The Book of Fairies
First published in Great Britain by George Newnes in 1924
Dean edition published in 2007

The Book of Pixies
First published in Great Britain by Dean in 1989

The Book of Brownies
First published in Great Britain by Geroge Newnes in 1924

This edition published 2015 by Dean,
an imprint of Egmont UK Limited
The Yellow Building, 1 Nicholas Road, London W11 4AN

ISBN 978 0 6035 7058 2
58962/2

www.egmont.co.uk

CONTENTS

Stories from The Book of Fairies

Stories from The Book of Pixies

Stories from The Book of Brownies

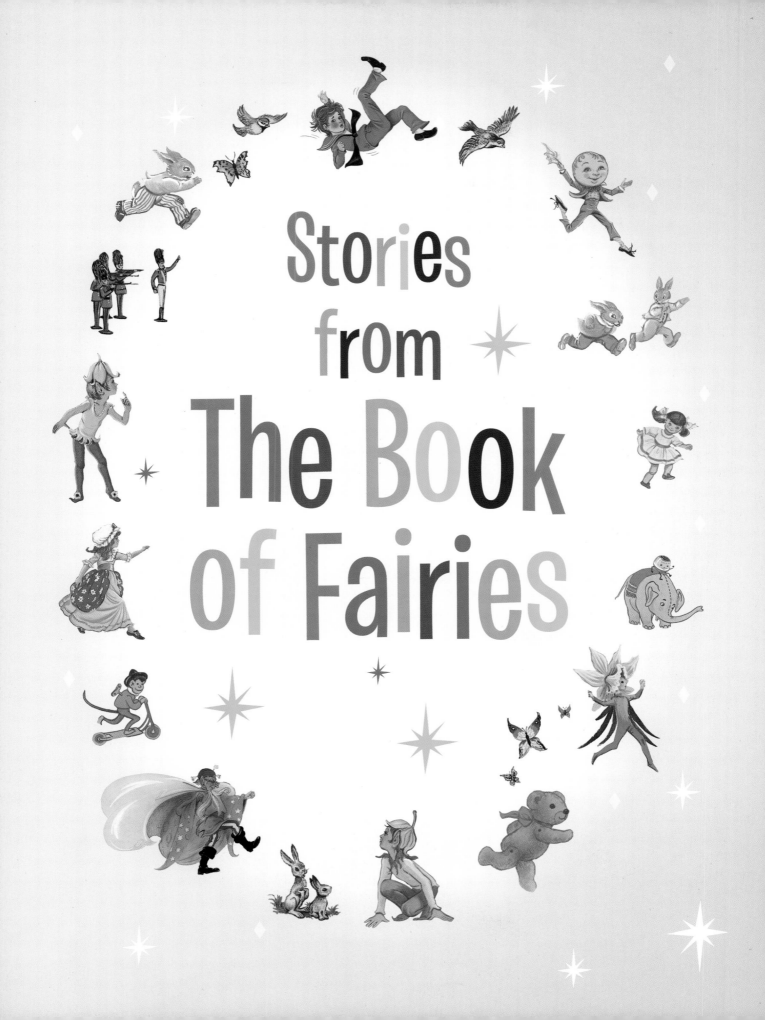

Stories from
The Book
of Fairies

Fireworks in Fairyland

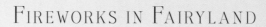

Once upon a time there lived in Fairyland a number of little workmen, all dressed in bright green. They had very long legs and very sleepy eyes, and they sat in the grass all day to do their work.

They were the fairies' knife-grinders, and whenever a fairy wanted her knife sharpened you could hear the buuzz-z-z of the blunt knife held

against the little grindstone that each workman had by him.

The fairies used to bring their knives each morning early, and then, as they were being sharpened, they sat on toadstools and talked.

'The North Wind is in a terrible temper today,' said one. 'I met him just now.'

'Ah!' said one of the knife-grinders. '*I* know why. It's because the late roses came out yesterday in the Queen's garden, and she won't let the North Wind blow till they're over!'

'And he says he *must* blow, else he'll burst himself with keeping all his breath in,' went on another workman, stopping his grinding because he was so interested.

'Yesterday I saw Hoo, the White Owl, and he told me a lovely story about those three naughty little gnomes, Ding, Dong, and Dell,' began another fairy.

'Oh, do tell us!' begged all the workmen, stopping work at once to listen.

The fairy told them the story, and the workmen forgot all about their knives. When the story came to an end the sun was high in the sky, and it was nearly twelve o'clock.

'Oh, I'm so sleepy!' yawned a knife-grinder, lying down on his back.

'I *can't* finish these knives!' said another, and fell asleep beside his grindstone.

There those lazy little workmen slept soundly until four o'clock, when the Fairy Queen happened to come along, bringing a crowd of elves with her.

'Oh, your Majesty, look here!' cried one, pointing to a sleeping workman. 'He's fast asleep, and it's only four o'clock!'

'How disgraceful!' exclaimed the Queen. 'And look at all those blunt knives! They ought to have been sharpened long ago! Does this often happen?'

'We don't know,' answered the elves, 'but Hoo, the White Owl, lives near here, and could tell you.'

So Hoo was called and flew silently down to the Queen.

'Yes, your Majesty,' he said, in answer to her question, 'they are good little workmen, but terribly lazy. They are for ever talking with the fairies, and going to sleep any hour of the day.'

'Wake them up,' commanded the Queen to her elves. 'I can't stop to scold them, but you may stay behind and do it for me.'

The Queen flew on and left some of her elves behind.

'We'll give them a fright,' whispered the elves. Then each elf flew down beside a workman and

shouted a most tremendous shout in his ear. Then, quick as lightning, they hid themselves behind toadstools.

You should have seen those workmen jump! They all woke up at once, nearly jumped out of their skins, and looked all round in great terror.

'What was it?' they all cried.

Out came the elves from behind the toadstools, looking very stern.

'The Queen has just passed,' they said, 'and found you all asleep with your work not done. She is very cross indeed!'

But the workmen hardly listened. 'Was it *you* who woke us up like that?' they asked, looking very fierce.

'Yes, it was, and it serves you right!' answered the elves.

'Then you are very unkind, and we'll pull your ears!' shouted the workmen, rushing at the elves. But, quick as thought, they spread their wings, and flew away, laughing at the angry little knife-grinders.

'It's a *shame*!' stormed one. 'Those horrid little elves are *always* playing tricks on us and making us jump!'

'Can't we pay them back somehow and give *them* a fright?' asked another.

'Yes, let's! How could we make them jump just like they made us?'

'I've got a glorious idea!' said another. 'Let's go to the world of boys and girls and get some fireworks. It's November 5th tomorrow and there will be plenty about.'

'Yes, and go to the palace and play tricks on those elves with them!' cried all the other workmen, looking really excited.

So it was all arranged. Two workmen were sent off to get rockets, Catherine Wheels, Golden Rain, and jumping squibs from our world. They soon came back with a big sack full of them, and the knife-grinders made all their plans.

Next morning a message came to them from the Queen, saying they must all go to the palace that day, as she was holding a great party and dance for her elves, and wanted all the knives sharpened.

'That's better still!' cried the workmen, and hurried off at once.

They sharpened all the knives very quickly and then asked if they could help lay the table for the feast, and polish the floor for the dancing.

'Certainly!' answered the Head Steward. 'You are very good to help us.'

So those knife-grinders slipped into the banqueting hall, and began preparing their tricks.

They put some crackers in the dishes of sweets and chocolates and some in the middle of a big ice-cream pudding.

'I'm going to put Golden Rain fireworks among all these flowers round the hall!' called a busy workman. 'The elves always smell the flowers!'

'And I'm pinning Catherine Wheels on to the wall!' chuckled another. 'The elves won't know what they are, and they'll be sure to poke about and see!'

'Look, do look! I've had a glorious idea! I've tied rockets to the front legs of every chair! Won't those elves jump?' called another knife-grinder, looking most delighted.

'Isn't it *lovely*? Won't they be cross? They *will* be sorry they made us jump!' called all the workmen.

'Now we'd better hide somewhere and watch. We'll go behind those big curtains. Have you all got squibs in your pockets?' asked the biggest workman.

'Yes,' answered the rest.

'Now, all be quiet whilst I say some magic. We shall have to use some to make the fireworks go off directly anyone touches them.'

Everyone was quiet, and the leader sang some queer words.

'There!' he said. 'Now, directly anyone *touches*

those hidden fireworks, they'll all go off bang! Let's go and hide.'

The knife-grinders ran behind the long curtains, and there they waited till the guests came in to the party.

Soon the elves arrived, all in beautiful dresses and shiny wings. Then came the Queen, and gave the signal for the feast to begin.

Everything went well until an elf asked for some ice-cream pudding. For directly the Head Steward began to put a spoon into it, there came a most tremendous noise!

Crack! Splutter-crack!! Bang!!!

It was the cracker inside the pudding, gone off directly it was touched!

'Oh, oh! What is it?' gasped the Head Steward, looking very astonished.

Then suddenly—

Crack! Bang! Crack!

The elves were helping themselves to chocolates and sweets, and the crackers in the dishes were exploding!

How those elves jumped! And how the naughty little workmen laughed, behind the curtain.

'Someone has been playing tricks,' said the Queen, looking rather stern. 'If you have all finished, get down, and we will start dancing.'

The elves got down, and went into the dancing hall. The workmen followed, making sure no one saw them, and hid behind the curtains there.

'What glorious flowers!' cried the elves, and bent to smell the wonderful roses round the walls.

Fizzle-fizzle-fizz! Whizz-z-z!

Out shot Golden Rain, directly the fairies smelt the roses!

'Oh, what is it?' they cried, falling over one another in their haste to get away. 'It must be some new sort of caterpillar! Ugh, how horrid!'

'Yes, and what are those funny curly things on the walls?' asked the Queen.

An elf went up to a Catherine Wheel and poked it with his finger.

Whirr-r-r-r! Whirr-r-r-r!

The wheel spun round and round and shot off sparks!

'Oh, it's alive! it's alive! What is it, what is it?' shouted the elves, crowding together in frightened astonishment.

'Never mind,' said the Queen, looking sterner than ever. 'Begin your dancing.'

The elves began dancing round the room.

'Throw your jumping squibs on the floor!' whispered the biggest workman. 'That will make the elves jump!'

Quickly the squibs were thrown on the floor of the hall.

Crack! Splutter-jump! Crack! Jump!!

Those squibs were jumping all over the place!

'Oh! Get off my toe, you horrid thing!'

'Goodness me! Go away, go away!'

'Oh, oh, what are they? They jump us and won't let us dance!'

The elves were really frightened.

'Go and sit down,' commanded the Queen, 'and I will find out who has done these naughty things.'

The elves went to the chairs round the hall and sat down.

Whizz-z-z! Whoosh-sh-sh! Bang!!!

All the rockets tied to the chairs shot up in the air directly they were touched by the elves!

'Oh, oh!' cried the elves, nearly jumping out of their skins with fright.

'Keep where you are,' called the Queen, 'and see what else happens.'

Nothing happened, and the elves began to feel more comfortable.

'Lord High Chamberlain,' commanded the Queen, in a dreadfully stern voice, 'go and look behind those curtains over there.'

The Lord High Chamberlain stepped across and pulled the curtains aside.

And there were all the naughty little green workmen, looking very frightened indeed!

'Come here,' said the Queen.

They all came and stood in front of her throne.

'What do you mean by playing such naughty tricks on my elves?' she demanded.

'Please, your Majesty, they made *us* jump the other day, so we thought we'd make *them* jump,' answered the biggest workman.

'You know quite well that that's not the right thing to do at all,' said the Queen. 'I am quite

ashamed of you. You are not fit to be in Fairyland. You have spoilt our party and frightened all my elves.'

'Oh, please, we *are* sorry now,' sobbed the workmen, feeling very miserable.

'You don't do your work well and you are lazy,' said the Queen. 'I think it would do you good to do some jumping and stretch those long legs of yours a bit. I am going to punish you, and perhaps you will remember another time that I will have no one in my kingdom who does not do his work well and beautifully.'

'*Please* let us sharpen the fairies' knives for them,' begged the knife-grinders. 'We really *will* do it beautifully now.'

'Very well, you may still do that,' said the Queen, 'and as you are so fond of making people jump, you had better jump a lot too.'

She waved her wand.

And every little workman there turned into a green grasshopper!

'Go into the fields,' said the Queen, 'and do your work properly.'

All the green grasshoppers turned to go, stretched their long legs, and *jumped* out of the hall! Hop and a jump, and a jump, and out they went into the fields.

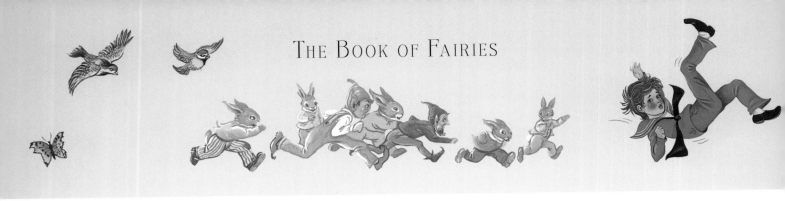

They still sharpen the fairies' knives for them, and you can hear their grindstones buzzing in the summer somewhere down in the grass. And when you see them hopping you will know why it is they jump instead of run!

Fireworks are forbidden in Fairyland, now, and I really don't wonder at it, do you?

Betty's
Adventure

There was once upon a time a little girl who didn't believe in fairies. 'But, Betty, there *are* fairies, because I've seen them,' said her brother Bobby.

'Pooh! You're telling stories!' answered Betty crossly. 'There aren't fairies, or gnomes, or elves, or anything like that, so you couldn't have seen any!'

Now the brownies heard her say this, and they determined to teach her a lesson.

'What can we do to show her she's wrong?' asked one.

'Don't you think it would be rather funny if we took her to the middle of Fairyland, where there's crowds of fairies and elves, and see what she says when she sees them?' laughed a merry little brownie.

'Yes, yes! Let's!' cried the others. So they made their plans and waited.

One day Betty was out for a walk by herself, when she saw a big notice up, which said: 'PLEASE DO NOT WALK THIS WAY.'

'How stupid!' said Betty. 'It doesn't look like a proper notice. I believe it's only a joke. Anyway, I *shall* go that way!'

'We thought she would! We thought she would!' chuckled the brownies, who had put up the notice and were hiding in the bushes.

Betty walked past the notice, and down a little lane. She came to a stream, and by the side of the bank rocked a little golden boat.

'There's no one here! I'll just get in and see how it feels to rock up and down like that!' said Betty. She jumped into the boat and sat down.

Out sprang the brownies, gave the boat a push, and ran back laughing.

Betty didn't see the brownies, and suddenly felt the boat jerk. Then it floated out into midstream, and began going down the river!

'Oh! Oh! Stop! Stop!' cried Betty, feeling frightened. But the boat wouldn't stop. It went by magic. Betty had no oars, and could do nothing.

Presently it passed cottages on each side. Old women in pointed black hats stood at the doors.

'They look just like witches in Bobby's story-book,' thought Betty, 'but I know they can't be.'

On and on the boat went, until Betty, tired with the sun, fell fast asleep. At last the boat stopped with a bump, and Betty woke up. She

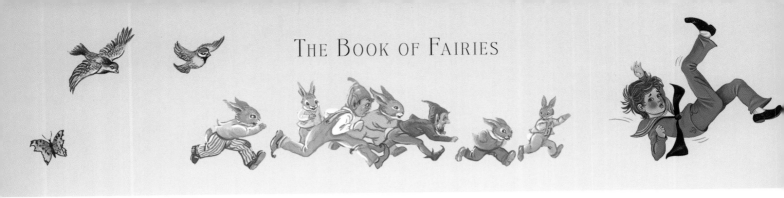

found the boat had stopped by some steps, so she got out and ran up them.

'Wherever am I?' she thought. Then she stared in astonishment. She saw a fairy dressed in blue, with long blue wings, coming towards her.

'It can't be a fairy!' thought Betty. 'It must be somebody dressed up for fun.'

'Welcome to Fairyland!' said the fairy.

'Don't be silly!' said Betty. 'There isn't such a place. And what are you dressed up like that for? Is there a fancy-dress party?'

The fairy looked puzzled. 'No,' she said, 'I'm

not dressed up. I'm just a fairy!'

'You're telling stories!' said Betty rudely. 'I shan't speak to you any more!' She walked on by herself, turned a corner, and came straight into a noisy market-place, full of fairies, elves, brownies, and gnomes.

'It *is* a fancy-dress party!' said Betty. 'Oh dear! I wish I'd got a fancy dress too, and had been invited!'

'Buy a magic spell?' asked a little brown gnome, running up to her with a tray full of curious packages.

'Oh, don't be silly!' said Betty, getting really cross. 'I know you're not real, so you needn't pretend to be! There aren't any fairies!'

All at once there fell a great silence. No one spoke, but everyone turned and looked at Betty in astonishment. Then a grandly dressed fairy, with great wings, stepped over to her.

'You must be making a mistake,' she said. 'You're in Fairyland, you know, and we think it is very bad manners, besides being very stupid, to say there aren't any fairies when you are surrounded by them.'

Betty began to feel alarmed. After all, it didn't really look like a fancy-dress party! Perhaps Bobby *was* right, and there *were* fairies!

But Betty was an obstinate little girl, and she hated to say she was wrong.

'I don't care *what* you say!' she said. 'I don't believe in fairies!'

The crowd round her looked angry.

'Call for Giant Putemright!' shouted someone, 'and put her in prison till she's a bit more polite!'

Betty felt frightened. She looked round for a way to escape, but there was none. Suddenly there was a shout!

'Here comes Giant Putemright!'

Betty looked and saw a great giant lumbering down the street. She saw everyone was looking at him, and not at her, and she turned and ran away as fast as she could. She ran and ran and ran, till she had no breath left. Then she turned and looked back. Far away she could see a crowd of little people, but they were going a different way.

'They won't catch me after all!' said Betty, sinking down on the grass for a rest. 'Oh dear! I don't like this adventure. I *wish* I'd never said I didn't believe in fairies. Why, here's hundreds and hundreds of them; all sorts!'

Just then she heard a little puffing noise. She looked up, and saw near by her a pair of railway lines, and over them was coming a tiny little train. It stopped near her, and the driver leaned out.

'Are you waiting for the train?' he called. 'We're going to the Glittering Palace.'

Betty jumped up. Yes! She would get in the train, then if the fairies tried to find her any more, she would be far away!

She scrambled into a little carriage and sat down on one of the cushions on the floor. There was a dwarf on another one, but he took no notice of her. The train whistled and went on again.

'What lovely country!' thought Betty as they went through fields of wonderful flowers and past gardens filled with roses.

'Oh! That's the Glittering Palace!' said Betty, as they came in sight of a great shining palace, with turrets and pinnacles gleaming in the sun.

The train stopped and Betty jumped out. 'I'd better ask the way home,' she thought. She went up to the driver.

'Could you tell me the way out of Fairyland?' she asked.

'No, I couldn't,' said the driver. 'But if you go and ask at the Glittering Palace, I dare say someone would tell you.' He blew the engine's whistle, waved to her, and drove away.

Betty made her way to the Glittering Palace. She came at last to some great open gates. There was no one to speak to, so she went through them

and up a great flight of steps. At the top she came to a big hall, hung with wonderful blue curtains.

'My goodness!' whispered Betty, stopping. 'Why, I do believe that's the Fairy Queen on that throne, that Bobby talks about such a lot.'

Sure enough it was! Around her was a crowd of fairies, and elves, all chattering excitedly.

'Silence!' said the Queen. 'Sylfai, you tell me what all this excitement is about.'

'If you please, your Majesty,' said Sylfai, 'there's a horrid little girl come to Fairyland, who doesn't believe in us! She's run away from us, and we thought we ought to come and tell you, so we all flew straight here!'

'Oh! Oh! There she is! There she is!' shouted an elf, pointing at poor Betty. She turned to run, but this time she was not quick enough, and the gnomes surrounded her, and dragged her to the Queen.

'Please! Please! I *do* believe in fairies!' wept Betty. 'I'm sorry I said I didn't.'

The Queen looked grave. 'You're a silly little girl,' she said. 'Because you can't leave Fairyland now! No one is allowed to if she comes here and disbelieves!'

'Isn't there any way of going back?' asked Betty. 'I didn't *mean* to come.'

'Yes, there's just one way,' said the Queen. 'And that is this: If you know anyone who really *does* believe in fairies, and loves them, he can take you back!'

'Oh, Bobby does, Bobby does!' cried Betty. 'Please bring him here!'

The Queen looked at her. 'Are you quite sure he does?' she asked. 'Because we don't want *two* people here who don't believe.'

'Yes, he *does*, he's always talking about you, and how he loves you!' said Betty.

The Queen turned to a gnome.

'Go and fetch Bobby!' she commanded. He sped off.

'Let's have a dance while we're waiting,' said a fairy. And they all began dancing in the hall, while the Queen looked on. Suddenly Betty gave a cry of delight.

'Bobby! Bobby!' she called.

And there was dear old Bobby, coming up the hall with the little gnome. He looked delighted to be with the fairies, but most astonished to find Betty there.

Betty told him all her adventures and begged him to take her home again.

'Of course I will, if the Queen will let me,' he answered.

'Yes, take Betty home!' said the Queen. 'She has learnt her lesson, but I am sorry she has not had a happy time in Fairyland. Still, it was her own fault. Will you bring her again, Bobby, the next time we have a party, and we'll try to make her love us, as well as believe in us.'

'I'd *love* to!' said Bobby, smiling in delight. 'What fun! Now then, Betty, hold on to me! I know the way home. Shut your eyes, turn round twice—One, two, three!' and down came a great wind, picked them up and set them down in their very own garden.

Betty rubbed her eyes. 'Oh, Bobby!' she said. 'I'm so glad you fetched me. I'll always love the fairies now, and oh! won't it be fun to go to their next party?'

'Let's go and tell Mummy,' said Bobby excitedly. 'My word, *what* an adventure!'

Bufo's
One-Legged
Stool

Once upon a time the King of Fairyland called all his fairy subjects to his palace. They came flying and running in great excitement, wondering why his Majesty should want them.

The King sat on his beautiful, shining throne, waiting until every fairy was there. Then he held up his hand for silence and spoke to them.

'Fairy-folk,' he began, 'once every year a prize is given to the fairy who thinks of the cleverest idea to make the world more beautiful. Last year, you remember, Morfael won the prize with his golden polish for the buttercups.'

'Yes, we remember!' shouted the fairies.

'Well, this year, I'm going to make a change,' said the King. 'I am going to give the prize to the one who thinks, not of the *cleverest* idea, but of the *most useful!* And please tell the rabbits and frogs and birds about it, because it's quite likely they would think of a good idea just as much as you fairy-folk.'

Well, the fairies were most excited. They rushed off telling everyone about it.

'I'm going to think hard for a whole week!' said one.

'And I'm going to use some old magic that will tell me the most useful thing in the world!' said another.

'Let's go and tell all the animals,' shouted a third.

So they visited the grey rabbits and told them. They called out the news to the grasshoppers. They gave the message to Hoo, the White Owl of Fairyland, and he promised to tell all the other birds.

'Now I do believe we've told everyone!' said the fairies.

'No, we haven't. What about ugly old Bufo the Toad, who lives on the edge of Fairyland?' asked an elf.

'Pooh! What's the good of telling *him*?' cried a pixie scornfully. 'He's so stupid and ugly, he'd *never* think of any good idea. Leave him alone!'

But it happened that next door to Bufo lived a brownie called Bron. He had decided to make a beautiful scarf for fairies to wear when the wind was cold. He thought it would be most useful. He was making it of spiders' webs and thistledown, and as he sat in his little garden at work, he sang a little song:

'Oh! I am very wise,
I'm sure to win the prize,
And when I've won the prize, you'll see
How very, very pleased I'll be!'

Bufo the Toad kept hearing him sing this and at last he got so curious that he crawled out of his cottage and asked Bron what prize he was singing about.

Bron told him. 'The King's giving a prize to anyone bringing him the most *useful* idea this year!' he explained. 'Why don't you try, Bufo?'

'I'm so clumsy!' said Bufo. 'But I'd like to try all the same. Yes, I think I will.'

'I'm making a wonderful scarf for when it's cold!' said Bron proudly. 'It's made of cobwebs and thistledown!'

'My! You are clever!' said Bufo. 'Now I'm going indoors and try to think of something myself!'

He waddled indoors. His cottage was very queer inside. Bufo was so fat and heavy that he had broken all the chairs and his sofa, through sitting on them too hard! So there were none in his cottage at all. He had a big table, and as he really did want something to sit on, he had made himself one large stool. He was so stupid at making things, that he

thought he had better give his stool just one large fat leg in the middle. He was afraid that if he tried to make three legs to it like Bron's smart little stool, he would never get them the same length. So inside his cottage there was only one table and a queer one-legged stool.

Bufo the Toad climbed up on to his stool, shut his great yellow eyes, and thought!

At last he opened his eyes. 'I've got an idea!' he cried. 'I'll make an eiderdown of pink rose petals! That will be a most useful thing, and it will smell lovely!'

So he hopped out into his garden and collected all the largest rose petals he could find. Then he begged some spider-thread from a spider friend and began.

But poor Bufo was clumsy. He kept breaking the spider's thread, and the wind blew half his rose petals away.

'Ha, ha!' laughed the rude little brownie. 'Ha, ha! Bufo! It really is a funny sight to see a great toad sewing rose petals! Don't you worry your stupid old head! *I'm* going to win the prize, I tell you!'

But Bufo wouldn't give up. He went and sat on his stool again and thought. He thought for three days before he found another idea.

That was really rather a good one. He caught a little pink cloud, and decided to stuff a pillow with it. He thought it would be so lovely and soft for fairies' heads.

Bron laughed to see Bufo poking the pink cloud into a big white pillowcase with his great fingers. He called his friends and they came and watched Bufo and teased him.

'Poke it a bit harder, Bufo!' they called over the fence. 'It's a naughty little cloud, isn't it? It won't let you win the prize.'

Bufo took no notice for a whole day. Then he

suddenly got angry, left the half-stuffed pillow on the grass, and hopped to the fence to smack the rude little brownies.

But alas! As soon as the half-stuffed pillow had no one to hold it, the little pink cloud began to rise in the air, to go back to the sky, and it took Bufo's lovely pillow-case with it!

'Oh, oh, now look what you've made me do!' wept Bufo, trying to jump into the air and catch the pillow. But he couldn't, and the naughty little brownies laughed harder than ever.

Bufo went and sat on his stool again. This time he thought for six weeks. When another idea came, he was so stiff with sitting that he could hardly jump off his stool.

'I'll make some wonderful blue paint, to paint the Queen's carriage with!' he decided. 'I know it wants repainting, so that will be useful.'

He lumbered off with a huge sack. He got the dawn fairies to give him a scraping off the blue of the sky. He asked the blue butterflies for a little powder off their wings. He took one bluebell flower and one harebell. Then he lumbered home again with his sack full of all these things.

When he got indoors, he took a blue shadow, mixed it with honey and water, and poured it into a large paint-pot. Then he emptied his sack

into it, and stirred everything up well.

'It's the most glorious blue paint ever I saw!' said Bufo, very pleased. '*This* will be useful, I know.'

Now the next day was the day the King had arranged to hold a meeting to judge all the ideas, and everyone in Fairyland was most excited. When the day came, Bufo put his paint outside his cottage door, all ready to take, and then began tidying himself up. Suddenly he heard a terrible yell from Bron, his next door neighbour.

'Help! Help! Arran the Spider is stealing my lovely scarf!'

Bufo rushed out to help, and saw Arran running off with Bron's scarf. He quickly stopped the spider, and took the scarf away.

'He stole some of my thread,' grumbled Arran, running off, frightened. 'I thought I'd come and punish him!'

'Oh, thank you for helping me,' cried Bron. 'If he'd taken my scarf, I wouldn't be able to win the prize.'

'Yes, but it's wrong to take Arran's thread, if he didn't want you to,' said Bufo severely. 'You ought to say you're sorry to him, and give it back!'

He waddled back to his cottage, but, oh! he quite forgot he had put his pot of blue paint outside the door. He walked straight into it, and

splish-splash! clitter-clatter! It was all upset.

'Oh! Oh! My beautiful paint!' wept Bufo. 'I've spilt it all, and there's no more time to think of other ideas!'

Some fairies passing by stopped to listen.

'You must take *something*, Bufo,' they called mischievously. 'The King will be cross with you if you don't.'

Bufo believed them. 'Oh dear! Will he really? But what *shall* I do? I've nothing else but my stool and a table!'

'Take the stool, Bufo!' laughed the fairies, flying on.

So poor old Bufo the Toad went indoors and fetched his one-legged stool, and joined the crowd of flying fairies. How they laughed to see him waddling along carrying a big one-legged stool.

At last they all reached the palace, and the King soon came to hear and to see the useful ideas that the fairy-folk had brought.

'Here's a wonderful necklace made of raindrops!' cried a fairy, kneeling before the King.

'It is beautiful, but not useful!' answered the King gently. 'Try again.'

'Here's a new sort of polish for the sunset sky!' said the next fairy.

The King looked at it. 'That's no better than

the one we use now,' he said. 'Next, please.'

Fairy after fairy came, and rabbits and birds and other animals.

Some had beautiful ideas that weren't useful, some had stupid ideas, and some had good ones.

At last Bron's turn came. He showed his beautiful scarf.

'It is lovely, Bron,' said the King, 'but it is not warm enough to be useful. Also I know you have been unkind to Bufo, and you took Arran's thread without asking. I am not pleased with you. Go away, and do better!'

Bron hung his head and crept away, blushing and ashamed.

At last everyone had shown their ideas, except Bufo. He crawled up to the King and put his one-legged stool down.

'I thought of many ideas, but they all got spoilt,' he said. 'Is this one any use? It is a good strong stool, easy to make, and quite nice-looking.'

The King looked at it thoughtfully. Then the Queen leaned forward and spoke.

'Don't you think, Oberon,' she said, 'that it is just the thing we want to put in the woods for fairy seats? Think how easy, too, they would be to put up in a ring for a dance!'

'Well now, so they would!' said the King. 'It

really is just what we want. It is certainly the most useful idea we've had given to us today. We could *grow* these one-legged stools by magic in the woods, and use them for tables *or* for stools!'

'Then we'll give Bufo the prize!' said the Queen. 'Three cheers for Bufo!'

How surprised the fairies were to see ugly old Bufo win the prize! And oh! how delighted Bufo was! He could hardly believe his ears. He almost cried with joy. He was given a little golden crown to wear, and though he certainly looked rather queer in it, he didn't mind a bit, because

he was so very proud of having won it!

One-legged stools were put all about the woods that very day, and they have been used ever since by fairy-folk. Sometimes you find them growing in a ring, and then you'll know there has been a dance the night before.

They are still called toadstools, although it is many, many years ago since Bufo the Toad won the prize. Not many people know why they have such a funny name, but you will be able to tell them the reason now, won't you?

The Wizard's
Magic Necklace

'Oh dear, oh dear!' sighed Gillie. 'I do wish I wasn't so ugly. My nose is so long and my brown suit is so old!'

Gillie looked at himself in a clear pool of water. He was a little gnome living in Fairyland, and he certainly *was* very ugly.

'Hullo, Gillie!' suddenly called a little voice.

Gillie looked round. He saw his friend the grey rabbit, sitting down among the primroses.

'Hullo, Greyears!' he said. 'What have you come to see me for?'

'I've got a letter for you,' said Greyears. 'It's to say that the rabbits are giving a party tonight, and they want you to come to it. The pixies are coming too, so be sure and look your best, won't you?'

Gillie took the letter and read it.

'How lovely!' he cried. 'Thank you so much for asking me. But, oh dear, I *wish* I wasn't so ugly, Greyears!'

'Yes, you are rather ugly,' said Greyears, looking at his friend. 'But if you bought a new coat, Gillie,

and wore some beads or something, you would look *much* nicer.'

'I can't have a new suit yet,' sighed Gillie. 'I've got to wait till next month. And I haven't any beads at all, have you?'

'No,' answered Greyears. 'But, I say, Gillie! I've got an idea!'

'What is it? Do tell me,' begged Gillie.

'Well, come over here, and I'll whisper,' said the grey rabbit, looking round to make sure that no one was about.

'Listen. You know where that old wizard Coran lives, don't you? Well, he has got a wonderful necklace. It is all made of yellow and red-brown stones. It would look simply *lovely* on your brown suit, Gillie.'

'Oh,' said Gillie, 'but he wouldn't lend it to me, I know. He's a dreadfully cross wizard.'

'Well, if you like, I'll get it for you. I can burrow into the room where he keeps it, and then bring it to you. He will never know. You can easily put it back when you've worn it,' said Greyears.

'All right,' answered Gillie. 'It's very nice of you, Greyears, and I shall look lovely at the party.'

'I'll bring it to you tonight, by this little pool,' called Greyears, hopping off as fast as he could.

Gillie felt very excited. He took off his little brown suit and mended up the holes beautifully with some spider's thread. He washed off a dirty mark and put it in the sun to dry. Then he sat down by the little pool and waited for Greyears to come back with the necklace.

'How lovely I shall look with a string of yellow and brown stones,' he thought. 'Oh, here comes Greyears.'

Greyears lolloped up to Gillie. He held a glittering necklace in his teeth.

'Oh, Greyears, how beautiful!' cried Gillie, taking it into his hands. 'See how the stones shine and glitter. Oh, how beautiful I shall be!'

'Sh!' said Greyears. 'Don't talk so loudly, I believe the old wizard heard me. Put on the necklace and come to the party with me, before he finds out it is gone.'

Off they both went, and Gillie had a most glorious evening dancing with the pixies. Everyone thought he looked lovely in his beautiful necklace, and he was very happy.

'It *has* been lovely,' said Gillie to the grey rabbit as they went home.

'Hark, what's that?' suddenly whispered Greyears.

They both crouched down in some bracken and

listened. They heard a curious noise—a sort of panting and groaning.

'It's the wizard,' whispered Greyears.

'Oh dear! Has he missed his necklace?' asked Gillie. 'Whatever shall I do? He'll be dreadfully angry if he finds me here wearing it.'

'Keep still,' said Greyears, 'and perhaps he won't find us.'

They both kept quite still, and presently along came the wizard with his servants. He stopped just by Greyears and Gillie.

'Now then,' he cried to his servants in a queer, panting voice. 'Now then, hurry up and do what I tell you. That necklace *must* be found. You must search in all the homes of the little gnomes for it.'

'Yes, your Excellency,' replied the servants.

'I feel sure one of them has got it. Oh dear! Oh dear! I'm much too old to come out at this time of night, all in the dark!' said the wizard, groaning, as he hobbled off away from the bracken where Gillie and Greyears were hiding.

They waited till he was safely out of sight, then they crept from the bracken and looked around. The necklace glittered in the starlight, and Gillie wondered what to do with it.

'Oh dear!' he sighed. 'How I wish I hadn't borrowed it. Now I must hide it somewhere till

the old wizard has forgotten about it, and then put it back somehow.'

'Where will you hide it?' asked Greyears. 'Don't you think it would be better to go and give it to the wizard and say you're sorry?'

'Oh no! I *couldn't!*' said Gillie. 'I should be so afraid he would be cross with me.'

'Shall I hide it in my burrow for you, Gillie?' asked the grey rabbit.

'No thank you—I know of a much better place. Come with me, Greyears, and I'll show you.' And off went the two friends as fast as they could.

At last they came to an old mossy wall. Gillie climbed up, right to the top, and sat there to get his breath.

'There's a big hole here, Greyears,' he called, 'and I'm going to hide the necklace in it.'

'Can I do anything to help you?' asked Greyears.

'Yes, scrape up some earth with your hind legs, and I'll fill the hole with it so that no one can see the necklace shining, if they fly over the wall.'

Greyears busily scraped some earth loose. Presently Gillie climbed down, and taking off his brown cap he filled it with earth. Then he climbed up again to the top of the wall.

'That's just enough,' he said; 'it covers the necklace nicely.'

'Plant some flowers along the top!' said Greyears, 'then no one will guess what's underneath.'

'How clever you are!' exclaimed Gillie, scrambling down again. He looked about for some flowers, and found some tiny white ones with four petals, growing in a hedge. He pulled them up by the roots and climbing up the wall again, he planted them all carefully along the top. Then he slid down to the ground.

'There! *That's* done!' he said. 'Thank you for helping me, dear Greyears. Now, let's go home, I'm so tired.'

'You can fetch the necklace in a month's time,' said Greyears, 'and put it back again somehow.'

Gillie went to Greyear's burrow for the night, and soon they were both sound asleep.

Gillie didn't go near the old wall at all for a long time. If he had, he would have seen something wonderful happening.

The little white flowers he planted were growing, and were spreading all along the wall— but they were no longer white! They were growing to be great strong flowers, yellow and red-brown like the necklace. They were beautiful in the sun, with their deep colours and soft, velvety petals. They smelt so sweet that some fairies flying by stopped to look at them.

'What lovely flowers!' cried one. 'I've never seen any like them before.'

'And how *did* they come to be growing there!' said the other. 'What a funny place to grow. Let's ask the Queen if she has heard of them?'

But when the Queen came *she* didn't know either, and was very puzzled, because of course she knew the names of all the flowers there were in Fairyland.

'They must be magic flowers,' she said at last. 'Bring the old wizard here, and ask him if *he* knows what they are.'

The old wizard was brought, groaning and panting, and leaning on a strong stick. Just behind came Gillie and Greyears, curious to know what everyone was looking at. They were most astonished to find sturdy yellow and brown flowers growing on the wall.

'Good afternoon, Sir Wizard,' said the Queen. 'Can you kindly tell me what those flowers are, up there on the wall?'

The wizard looked.

'Good gracious me,' he cried, 'they're exactly the colour of my lost necklace! That means that they are planted over it, for the stones are magic, and would turn the flowers to yellow and red-brown like themselves.'

'Dear me,' said the Queen, 'but whoever could have put the necklace there?'

'Oh, please, your Majesty, *I* did,' said Gillie, kneeling down in front of the Queen, and beginning to cry. He told her all about the party and how he borrowed the necklace.

'But whatever did you want a necklace for?' asked the Queen.

'Because I am so ugly, and I thought it would make me look lovely,' sobbed Gillie.

'Why, Gillie, you've a *dear* little face!' said the Queen kindly. 'Tell the wizard you're sorry, and I

expect he'll forgive you, now he knows where his necklace is.'

'Oh yes, I'll forgive Gillie,' grunted the wizard. 'Only you must climb up and get my necklace for me again.'

'Yes, I will,' cried Gillie, climbing up the wall, and sitting among the flowers.

'What shall we call those lovely flowers?' said the Queen.

'Hm! I should call them *wall*-flowers,' growled the wizard, 'because of where they're growing.'

'Yes, we will,' said the Queen. 'That's a good idea.'

And we still call them wallflowers wherever they grow—on the top of a wall, or in the garden beds—and there are some people who call them '*Gillie* flowers,' because they remember the naughty little gnome who, years ago, planted the flowers on the wall to hide the necklace of yellow and brown, and so made the very first wallflowers grow.

The Lost
Golden Ball

There was great excitement in Fairyland. The Queen's heralds had just gone through the streets of the chief town, and blown on their silver trumpets, to say that every fairy was to go to the big market-place, and wait there for the Queen to come.

'Oyez, oyez, oyez!' they cried. 'Her Majesty wishes to speak with you all at half-past nine this morning!'

'What *can* it be about!' cried the excited fairies, gathering here and there in little crowds. 'Perhaps someone's been naughty. Or perhaps the Queen wants us to do something for her!'

'Ding, dong, ding, dong!' chimed all the bluebells suddenly.

'Quarter-past nine!' called the fairies to each other. 'Come along to the market-place, everybody. The Queen will be coming in a few minutes!'

Off flew fairies and elves, and off ran pixies, gnomes, and brownies as fast as ever they could. Presently a great crowd was gathered in the marketplace, all wondering what their Queen wanted them for.

'Ding, dong, ding, dong! Ding, dong, ding, dong!' chimed the bluebells round about.

'Half-past nine! Here she comes! Isn't she beautiful? Hip, hip, hurrah!' cheered the fairies as the Queen flew down to the throne set high in the middle of the market-place.

'Good-day to you all!' she said, in her clear silvery voice, when all the fairies were quiet and not a sound could be heard. 'I have come to ask your help. You all know that the Prince of Dreamland has been staying here, and has lately gone back to his own country.'

'Yes, yes, your Majesty!' answered the listening fairies.

'He carried with him a bright golden ball which had, closely hidden inside it, the secret of a new magic spell. It is a wonderful spell which he hoped would make his ill Princess well again. You all know she has been ill?'

'Yes, your Majesty, and we are very sorry,' called the fairies.

'On his way home,' went on the Queen, 'his carriage was drawn by six white rabbits. Suddenly a dog began barking in the distance, and the rabbits were so frightened that they ran away, and in their fear upset the carriage. In the confusion and muddle the golden ball was lost, and the

Prince of Dreamland cannot find it anywhere. Will you help to find it?'

'Oh yes, we'd love to, your Majesty!' answered all the fairies in great excitement.

'Very well. Go now, and seek for it,' commanded the Queen. 'You must find it today, for the spell inside the ball will be no use tomorrow. It must be used before the moon is full.'

Off went all the fairies, helter-skelter, through the woods and lanes.

'I shall look in all the long grass!' said Fairy Rosemary. 'I am sure I shall find it!'

'*I* shall look in all the little pools!' said a yellow pixie. 'It might easily have rolled into one, and be hidden there! Come along and help me, pixie-folk!'

'*We* are going to hunt in the squirrels' nests!' shouted the frolicking elves. 'We think the squirrels might have found it and hidden it!'

'Where are *you* going to look, Karin?' shouted the brownies, speaking to an ugly little gnome who was sitting on a mossy stone, thinking.

'I think I shall look under the gorse bushes,' said Karin.

'Pooh! Fancy looking there! You'll get pricked all over. You *are* a silly-billy,' sang the brownies, dancing round Karin and laughing.

Karin hated being laughed at. He was a shy

little gnome, ugly and clumsy. He couldn't do the dainty things his comrades did. He looked so funny when he tried to dance, that, although the fairies tried not to, they simply *couldn't* help laughing. And when he began to sing, everybody flew away as fast as they could. This hurt him very much.

'Why don't they love me and want to be with me?' he used to think sadly, going off by himself.

He was too shy to ask the other fairies and gnomes to be his friends and to like him. He was *much* too shy to tell them he loved them, and as nobody ever guessed what he thought, Karin was always left alone, for everyone thought he was cross and surly, and didn't want to make friends.

'Oh dear!' said Karin sadly to himself, as the brownies ran off to look for the golden ball. 'Why does everybody laugh at me and nobody want me to come with them. I *wish* I wasn't ugly and stupid!'

He wandered off by himself, looking for a gorse bush to peep underneath. He found one, and lay down in the grass to wriggle underneath it. It was very prickly and very horrid.

'Ha, ha, ha! Ho, ho, ho!' suddenly laughed someone. 'Karin the Gnome, what in the world

are you doing? Do you want to find out if prickles are prickly?'

'Bother!' thought Karin, wriggling out again. 'Someone or other is *always* laughing at me.'

He sat up on the grass and brushed away the bits of gorse that had clung to him. Then he looked to see who had spoken.

It was Hoo, the White Owl. He was sitting on a hazel tree, and looking very much amused.

'It isn't nice of you to laugh at me,' said Karin. 'I hate being laughed at. I was only looking for the golden ball that the Prince of Dreamland lost.'

'A golden ball!' said Hoo. 'Well, now I believe *I* know where that is.'

'Oh, do tell me!' begged Karin excitedly. 'You can't *think* how I'd love to take it to the dear Queen.'

'Well, I'm sorry I laughed at you just now, if you didn't like it,' said Hoo. 'And to show you I'm sorry I'll tell you where I saw the golden ball.'

'Oh, thank you, thank you!' said Karin gratefully. 'Whisper in my ear, Hoo.'

So Hoo flew down and whispered in Karin's ear. 'As I flew by the heath the other night, I saw something gleaming in the moonlight. It was rolling along by itself, and I knew it was magic. I watched where it went, and I saw it roll down beneath a silver birch tree, under a piece of bracken by the bank where Greyears the rabbit lives. You will find it there!'

'Thank you, *ever* so much,' said Karin, jumping up excitedly.

'Tu-whit, tu-whit, don't mention it,' called Hoo, flying off silently into the trees.

'Hurrah! Hurrah! I'll find the ball! What fun!' thought Karin, running as hard as he could over the grass. The bank where Greyears lived was a long long way away, and he knew he would have to hurry.

He came to the heath. It was a big common called Hampstead Heath, stretching away in the distance. To Karin's surprise it was packed with crowds and crowds of people, some walking, some sitting, and some picnicking.

He hid behind a tree and watched. Although he didn't know it, it was Whit-Monday and everyone had come out into the sunshine, away from the shops, away from the busy towns, and from the stuffy offices. There were children everywhere, running, laughing and playing. Mothers sat here and there and fathers played cricket with the boys.

'Dear me, what a crowd of people!' thought Karin, 'and how happy they all look!'

He watched them for some time, then decided he must go on his way. He slipped from bush to bush and tree to tree, unseen, wrapping his green cloak closely round his red jacket and brown knickers. He passed many groups of happy children on his way across the heath, but none of them saw him.

As he glided behind a gorse bush, he stopped suddenly and slipped to the other side. There was a little girl behind it, sitting on the grass and crying. He didn't want her to see him. He was going on his way, when an extra large sob from the little girl stopped him.

'I wonder what's the matter with her!' said Karin to himself, peeping round the bush.

She was a dear little girl. She had short curly hair, big blue eyes filled with tears, and a crying, drooping mouth.

'I want my Mummy,' she kept saying. 'I want my Mummy! I'm so lonely, I *do* want my Mummy!'

Here was somebody else who was lonely besides Karin, and Karin, who knew how miserable it was to feel lonely was dreadfully sorry for the little girl. He wondered if his ugly face would frighten her if he spoke to her. He decided to try.

He slipped out from behind the gorse bush and stood in front of her. She looked up, surprised.

'Oh,' she said, 'what a *dear* little man! I'm sure you're a fairy, aren't you?'

Karin was so astonished to hear anyone call him a *dear* little man that he couldn't say anything, but just stood and smiled delightedly.

The little girl put up her hand and stroked him. 'I'm *so* glad to see you,' she said. 'I was just wishing a fairy or something would come and help me.'

'What's the matter with you?' asked Karin, finding his voice at last. 'I heard you crying!'

'Well, I'm lost!' said the little girl, her eyes filling with tears again. 'I'm Ann, and I've lost my

Mummy in all that crowd, and I can't find her.'

'I'm so sorry,' said Karin.

'But you'll find her for me, won't you?' said the little girl, cheering up. 'Fairies can do anything, you know!'

Karin stared at her. 'I'm afraid I can't stop any longer!' he said. 'You see, I'm doing something very important today. Else I *would* have stopped.'

The little girl began to cry again. 'Aren't I important too?' she sobbed. 'You aren't the nice kind fairy I thought you were. I'm *s'prised* at you. I really am!'

Karin couldn't bear to see her cry. He sat down by her and put his arms round her.

'Don't cry, little girl,' he said, 'I'll give my important business to somebody else to do, then I can stay and help you.'

'Oh, you *darling*,' said Ann, and kissed him. 'I love you ever-so.'

Karin was filled with delight to hear her say so. He never remembered hearing anyone say that to him before. He thought children must be simply lovely, if they went about loving everybody like that.

'I will be dreadfully disappointed not to find the golden ball and to let someone else get it,' he thought. 'But if this little girl wants me, I don't

mind giving up finding it—at least, I don't mind *very* much!'

He told Ann to stay where she was, and running to a pixie he saw by some bracken, he shouted to him:

'Hoo told me where the golden ball was. It's under the bracken by the birch tree growing near the bank where Greyears lives!'

At once the pixie darted off delightedly, and Karin returned to the little girl.

'I've told someone else my important business,' he said. 'Now, tell me what your mother's like and I'll go and find her.'

'She's got curly brown hair and kind eyes,' said Ann, 'and she's got a lovely purple hat with big red roses on it, and a purple coat!'

'Oh, I'll be sure to find her easily,' said Karin. 'Stay here till I come back.'

'I'll eat my dinner while you're gone,' said Ann, opening a little basket of sandwiches. 'Would you like some to take with you?'

'No, thank you,' said Karin. 'I don't think I should like your food very much. You eat it all yourself!'

'You *are* a kind little man,' said Ann, giving him a hug. 'I really think you've got the kindest face I ever saw.'

Karin was so delighted to hear anyone praise his ugly face and call it kind, that he almost shouted for joy. He ran off happily.

He searched and searched for a long time, but nowhere did he see a lady with a purple hat and red roses. There were plenty of red roses but no purple hats.

'Oh dear! Oh dear! I *must* find Ann's mother,' said Karin desperately. At last he went back to Ann, to see what she was doing.

She was fast asleep.

'I'll go and have another look,' said Karin, who was getting very tired of searching all over the crowded heath. 'I do hope I find her mother this time.'

As he wandered over the heath again, looking round him as he went, he suddenly saw a very sad-looking lady who was also looking all round *her* as she went. He looked at her hat. It was purple with red roses, and her coat was purple too! It must be Ann's mother.

Karin hurried up to her. 'Please,' he said, 'are you looking for Ann?'

'Yes, yes, I am!' answered the lady, not seeming at all surprised to see Karin. 'Oh, do you know where she is? Pray, pray take me to my little girl quickly! Is she all right?'

'Quite all right,' said Karin. 'Follow me.' He walked off quickly in the direction of Ann's gorse bush, and the mother followed closely behind. On the way a pixie popped his head from behind a piece of bracken and called to Karin:

'I went to the bank where Greyears lives, but I couldn't find the golden ball, Karin.'

'Oh, I'm sorry. I expect someone else found it!' answered Karin, hurrying on.

At last they reached the place where Ann was. She was just waking up. As she heard their footsteps, she looked up and saw her mother.

'Mummy! Mummy!' she cried, flinging herself into her mother's arms. 'Oh, Mummy, I'm so glad it's you. I lost you and I've been so lonely!'

The mother clasped her little girl close, as though she would never let her go, and kissed her curly head again and again.

'That dear, kind little man helped me!' said Ann. 'Oh, you dear fairy, I want to give you something. I found it this morning, and it's *ever* so pretty. I'd love to keep it for myself, but I want to give it to you because you've been so nice and I love you. Look!' and she took something from her little basket and held it out to Karin.

It was the Prince of Dreamland's lost golden ball!

'I found it under some bracken by a birch tree!' said the little girl. 'I want *you* to have it, Karin.'

Karin was so astonished and delighted that he could hardly say thank you. He gave Ann a hug, took the ball, said goodbye, and ran off as fast as he could, thinking that surely children were the very nicest things in all the world.

He ran and ran and ran, hoping he would get to the market-place where all the fairies were to meet, before it was too late. As he came near, he saw hundreds of fairy-folk gathered there and the Queen was speaking.

'Thank you all for looking,' she was saying. 'I am dreadfully sorry nobody found the golden ball, but I expect one of the crowd of people who came to Hampstead Heath today found it instead. I do wish I knew where it was.'

'Here it is! Here it is!' suddenly called an excited voice. All the fairies turned and saw Karin making his way to the Queen, holding in his right hand a wonderful golden ball.

'Karin! Karin's got it! Fancy, Karin's found it!' cried all the fairies to each other.

'Oh, Karin, how lovely!' said the Queen gladly. 'Where *did* you get it?'

Then Karin knelt down and told all the story of the day's happenings.

'You have done well!' said the Queen. 'You gave up something you wanted for the sake of a little girl, and lo and behold, the little girl gave you what you thought you had given up—the golden ball! It was a good reward for unselfishness. Now tell me, what wish shall I grant you for bringing me the golden ball!'

'Oh, please, your Majesty, let me go and play on Hampstead Heath with the children!' begged Karin. 'I believe they'd love me, and I *do* so want to be loved. I don't think they'd mind my ugly face. And I'd love to find their mothers for them when they're lost!'

The Queen smiled. 'We'll all love you, now we know you want to be loved,' she said. 'Yes, you may go and live on Hampstead Heath and look after the children there, Karin!'

And Karin can be found there to this very day. No child need fear being lost, for Karin will be sure to help him somehow, whether the child sees him or not! He is as happy as can be, for all the children love him, and he is happiest of all on Bank Holidays, for then he has so many children to look after, he hardly knows where to begin!

Pinkity and Old Mother Ribbony Rose

Once upon a time there lived an old witch called Mother Ribbony Rose. She kept a shop just on the borders of Fairyland, and because she sold such lovely things, the fairies allowed her to live there in peace.

She was very, very old, and very, very clever, but she wasn't very good. She was never kind to her neighbour, the Bee-Woman, and never helped the Balloon-Man, who lived across the road, and who was often very poor indeed when no one came to buy his lovely balloons.

But her shop was simply lovely. She sold ribbons, but they weren't just ordinary ribbons. There were blue ribbons, made of the mist that hangs over faraway hills, and sea-green ribbons embroidered with the diamond sparkles that glitter on sunny water. There were big broad ribbons of shiny silk, and tiny delicate ribbons of frosted spider's thread, and wonderful ribbons that tied their own bows.

The fairies and elves loved Mother Ribbony Rose's shop, and often used to come and buy there,

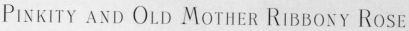

whenever a fairy dance was going to be held and they wanted pretty things to wear.

One day Mother Ribbony Rose was very busy indeed.

'Good morning, Fairy Jasmin,' she said, as a tall fairy, dressed in yellow, came into her shop. 'What can I get you today?'

'Good morning, Mother Ribbony Rose,'

answered Jasmin politely. She didn't like the old witch a bit, but that didn't make any difference, she was always polite to her. 'I would like to see the newest yellow ribbon you have, please, to match the dress I've got on today.'

Mother Ribbony Rose pulled out a drawer full of yellow ribbons. Daffodil-yellows, orange-yellows, primrose-yellows, and all shining like gold.

'Here's a beauty!' said she, taking up a broad ribbon. 'Would you like that?'

'No, thank you,' answered Jasmin, 'I want something narrower.'

The witch pulled out another drawer and scattered the ribbons on the counter.

'Ah, here's one I like ever so!' exclaimed Jasmin, lifting up a long thin piece of yellow ribbon, just the colour of her dress. 'How much is it?'

'Two pieces of gold,' answered Mother Ribbony Rose.

'Oh dear, you're terribly expensive,' sighed Jasmin as she paid the money and took the ribbon.

Mother Ribbony Rose looked at all the dozens of ribbons scattered over the counter.

'Pinkity, Pinkity, Pinkity,' she called in a sharp voice.

Out of the back of the shop came a tiny gnome.

'Roll up all these ribbons quickly, before anyone

else comes in,' ordered Mother Ribbony Rose, going into the garden.

Pinkity began rolling them up one by one. He did it beautifully, and so quickly that it was a marvel to watch him.

When all the ribbons were done, he went to the window and looked out. He saw fairies, gnomes, and pixies playing in the fields and meadows.

'Oh dear, dear, dear!' suddenly said Pinkity in a woebegone voice. 'How I would love to go and play with the fairies. I'm so *tired* of rolling up ribbons.' A large tear rolled down his cheek, and dropped with a splash on the floor.

'What's the matter, Pinkity?' suddenly asked a little voice.

Pinkity jumped and looked round. He saw a tiny fairy who had come into the shop and was waiting to be served.

'I'm so tired of doing nothing but roll up ribbons all day,' explained Pinkity.

'Well, why don't you do something else?' asked the fairy.

'That's the worst of it. I've never done anything else all my life but roll up ribbons in Mother Ribbony's shop, and I *can't* do anything else. I can't paint, I can't dance, and I can't sing! All the other fairies would laugh at me if I went to play

with them, for I wouldn't even know *how* to play!' sobbed Pinkity.

'Oh yes, you would! Come and try,' said the little fairy, feeling very sorry for the lonely little gnome.

'Come and try! Come and try *what?*' suddenly said Mother Ribbony's voice, as she came in at the door.

'I was just asking Pinkity if he would come and play with us,' answered the little fairy, feeling rather afraid of the witch's cross looks.

Mother Ribbony Rose snorted.

'Pinkity belongs to *me*,' she said, 'and he's much too busy in the shop, rolling up my beautiful ribbons all day, to have time to go and play with *you*. Besides, no one is allowed in Fairyland unless they can do some sort of work, and Pinkity can do nothing but roll up ribbons! I'm the only person who would keep him for that, for no one in Fairyland keeps a ribbon shop.' And the old witch pulled one of Pinkity's big ears.

'I should run away,' whispered the little fairy to Pinkity when her back was turned.

'I wish I could! But I've nowhere to run to!' whispered back Pinkity in despair.

At that moment there came the sound of carriage wheels down the cobbled street, and old

Mother Ribbony Rose poked her head out to see who it was.

'Mercy on us! It's the Lord High Chancellor of Fairyland, and he's coming here! Make haste, Pinkity, and get a chair for him!' cried the old witch, in a great flurry.

Sure enough it was.

The Chancellor strode into the shop, very tall and handsome, and sat down in the chair.

'Good morning,' he said. 'The King and Queen are holding a dance tonight, and they are going to make the wood gay with ribbons and hang fairy lamps on them. The Queen has asked me to come and choose the ribbons for her. Will you show me some, please?'

'Certainly, certainly, your Highness!' answered Mother Ribbony Rose, pulling out drawer after drawer of gay ribbons. Pinkity sighed as he watched her unroll ribbon after ribbon, and show it to the Chancellor.

'Oh dear! I'm sure it will take me hours and *hours* to roll up all that ribbon!' he thought to himself sadly.

'This is wonderful ribbon!' said the Chancellor admiringly. 'I'll have fifty yards of this and fifty yards of that. Oh, and I'll have a hundred yards of this glorious silver ribbon! It's just like moonlight.

And send a hundred yards of this pink ribbon, please, too, and I'll have a ribbon archway with mauve lamps made, leading from the Palace to the wood. The Queen will be delighted!'

'Certainly!' answered the witch, feeling excited to think of all the gold she would get for such a lot of ribbon. 'The pink ribbon is very expensive, your Highness. It's made of pink sunset clouds, mixed with almond blossom. I've only just got a hundred yards left!'

'That will just do,' said the Chancellor, getting up to go. 'Send it all to the Palace, please. And don't forget the *pink* ribbon, it's most important, *most* important!'

And off the Chancellor went to his carriage again.

Mother Ribbony Rose, who cared for gold more than she cared for anything else in the world, rubbed her hands together with delight.

'Now then, Pinkity!' she called. 'Come here and roll up all this ribbon I've been showing to the Chancellor, and measure out all that he wants!'

Pinkity began rolling up the ribbon. He did it as quickly as ever he could, but even then it took him a long time. He measured out all the many yards that the Chancellor wanted, and folded them

neatly. Then he got some paper and began to make out the bill.

'Hullo,' said Pinkity, 'the inkpot's empty. I must get the ink bottle down and fill it!'

He climbed up to the shelf where the big bottle of black ink was kept, and took hold of it.

But alas! Poor Pinkity slipped, and down fell the big bottle of ink on to the counter, where all the Chancellor's ribbon was neatly folded in piles! The cork came out, and before Pinkity knew what was happening all the ink upset itself on to the lovely ribbon, and stained it black in great patches.

In came old Mother Ribbony Rose.

'Pinkity! Pinkity! Look what you've done! And I haven't any more of that pink ribbon! You did it on purpose, I know you did, you naughty, naughty little gnome!' stormed the witch, stamping up and down.

Pinkity was dreadfully frightened. He was so frightened that, without thinking what he was doing, he jumped clean through the window and ran away!

He ran and ran and ran.

Then he lay down beneath a hedge and rested. Then he ran and ran and ran again, until it was night.

At last he came to a beautiful garden, lit by the

moon, and quite empty, save for lovely flowers. It was the Queen's garden, but Pinkity did not know it.

'I'm free! I'm free!' cried Pinkity, throwing his hat in the air. 'There's a dear little hole beneath this rock, and I'll hide there, and I'll NEVER go back to Mother Ribbony Rose.'

He crept beneath the rock, shut his eyes and fell fast asleep.

Next morning he heard fairies in the garden, and they were all talking excitedly.

'Yes, it was a naughty little gnome called Pinkity, who spoilt all the Queen's lovely ribbon,' said one fairy.

'Yes, and he did it on purpose, old Mother Ribbony Rose says. Just fancy that!' said another.

'And the Chancellor says if anyone catches him, they're to take him to the Palace to be punished, and given back to Mother Ribbony Rose,' said a third.

Pinkity lay and listened, and felt the tears rolling down his cheeks. He had so hoped that perhaps the fairies would help him.

All that day Pinkity hid, and at night he crept out into the lovely garden, and the flowers gave him honey to eat, for they were sorry for him.

For a long time Pinkity hid every day and only

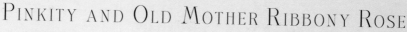

came out at night. One day he heard a group of fairy gardeners near by, talking hard.

'What *are* we to do about those little ferns?' they said. 'Directly they come up, their tiny fronds are spread out, and the frost *always* comes and bites them, and then they look horrid. It's just the same with the bracken over there!'

'It's so difficult to fold the fronds up tightly,' said the fern fairies. 'They *will* keep coming undone!'

'Well, we *must* think of something,' said the gardeners decidedly. 'The Queen simply loves her fernery, and she will be so upset if the frost bites the ferns again this year. Let's go and ask the rose gardeners if they can give us any hints.'

That night Pinkity went over to the baby ferns and bracken and looked at them carefully. It was a very frosty night, and they looked very cold and pinched.

'*I* know! I know!' cried Pinkity, clapping his hands. 'I'll *roll* them up like ribbons, and then they'll be quite warm and safe, and won't come undone till the frost is gone!'

So Pinkity started rolling each fern frond up carefully. It wasn't as easy as rolling ribbon, for the fronds had lots of little bits to tuck in, but he worked hard and managed it beautifully. The baby

ferns were very grateful, and so was the bracken.

'Thank you, thank you,' they murmured. 'We love being rolled up, and we're much warmer now.'

Pinkity worked all night, and just as daylight came, he finished the very last piece of bracken and ran back to his hole to hide.

At six o'clock along came the gardeners. They stared and stared and stared at the ferns.

'Whatever has happened to them!' cried they in amazement. 'They're rolled up just like ribbon!'

'What a splendid idea!' said the Head Gardener. 'But who did it? Someone very kind and very clever must have done it!'

'*Who* did it? *Who* did it?' cried everyone.

Pinkity, trembling with excitement, crept out of his hiding-place.

'If you please,' he said, '*I* did it!'

'Why, Pinkity! It's Pinkity, the naughty little gnome!' cried the fairies.

'I wasn't really naughty,' said Pinkity. 'The ink spilt by accident on the ribbon. I wouldn't have spoilt the dear Queen's ribbon for anything in the world.'

'Well, you've been so kind to our ferns,' said the fairies, 'that we believe you. But how *did* you learn to be so clever, Pinkity?'

'I'm not clever *really*,' said Pinkity, 'but I can roll up ribbons nicely—it's the only thing I *can* do—so it was easy to roll up the ferns.'

The fairies liked the shy little gnome, and took him in to breakfast with them. In the middle of

it in walked Her Majesty the Queen!

'*Who* has looked after my baby ferns?' she asked in a pleased voice.

'Pinkity has! Pinkity has!' cried the fairies, pushing Pinkity forward. Then they told the Queen all about him.

'It was quite an accident that your lovely ribbon was spoilt,' said Pinkity, 'and I was dreadfully sorry, your Majesty.'

'I'm quite *sure* it was an accident,' said the Queen kindly, 'and I have found out that all Mother Ribbony Rose cares about is gold, so I am sending her right away from Fairyland, and you need never go back!'

'Oh, how lovely!' cried Pinkity joyfully.

'Your Majesty! Let him look after the ferns and bracken, and teach other fairies how to roll up the baby ones!' begged the fairies. 'He *is* so clever at it.'

'Will you do that for us, Pinkity?' said the Queen.

'Oh, your Majesty, I would *love* it!' answered Pinkity joyfully, feeling happier than ever he had been in his life before.

He began his work that very day, and always and always now you will find that fern fronds are rolled up as tight as can be, just like the

ribbon Pinkity rolled up at the ribbon shop.

As for old Mother Ribbony Rose, she was driven right away from Fairyland, and sent to live in the Land of Deep Regrets, and nobody has ever heard of her since.

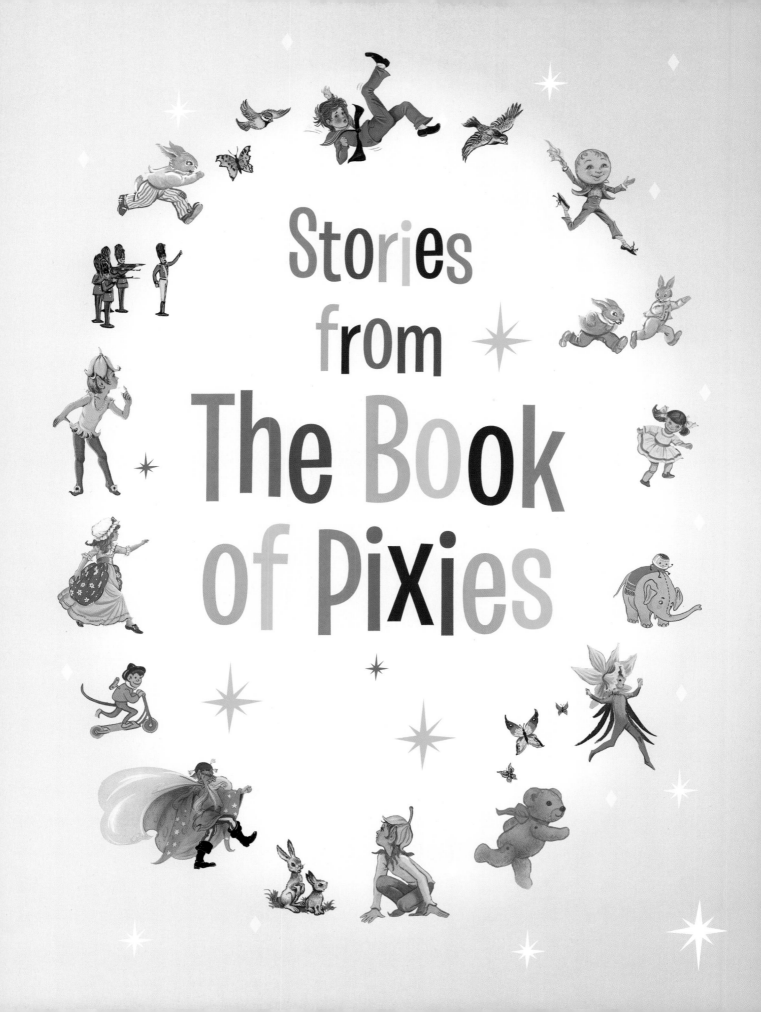

Stories from The Book of Pixies

The Three Wishes

Elsie and Bobby were sitting in the meadow, and, as usual, they were quarrelling.

They were brother and sister, but to hear them quarrelling with one another, you might have thought they were enemies!

'I didn't want to come to this wood. I wanted to go up the hill,' said Elsie. 'You always do what you want. You never do what I want.'

'Oh, you story-teller!' said Bobby. 'You are the most selfish girl I know – I'm always having to do what you choose. I don't like you a bit.'

'Well, I don't like—' Elsie began, and then she stopped. She had seen something moving in the buttercups near her. She put out her hand quickly and caught the thing that was moving.

To her enormous surprise, it was a pixie! The little creature gave a scream, and wriggled hard. But Elsie didn't let go. She held the little creature very tightly.

'Look!' she said to Bobby, in an excited voice. 'Look! I've caught a fairy!'

'Let me go!' squealed the little thing. 'You are hurting me.'

'Make her give us three wishes,' said Bobby, suddenly. 'Go on – tell her. We might get three wishes that would come true!'

Elsie squeezed the poor little pixie till she cried out.

'Give us three wishes and I'll let you go,' she said. 'Three wishes! Then we can make ourselves rich and happy and wise.'

'I'll give you three wishes,' said the pixie. 'But they won't do you any good! Children like you can't wish for the right things! But I'll give you three wishes if you want them.'

Elsie let the pixie go, and the little thing fled away among the bluebells, laughing as if she had heard a joke.

'What's she laughing at?' said Bobby. 'Oh, well, never mind. Now, what shall we wish?'

'I want to wish for a budgerigar that can talk,' said Elsie, at once. 'I've always wanted one.'

'What a silly wish!' said Bobby. 'No – let's wish for a little aeroplane that will take us anywhere we want to go.'

'I'm sure I don't want to fly in the air with you as the pilot,' said Elsie. 'No, you're not to wish that.'

'Well, I shall,' said Bobby, and he wished it. 'I wish I had a little aeroplane of my own, that I could fly off in.'

At once a most beautiful little aeroplane flew down from the air and landed beside Bobby. He was simply delighted. He got into it and grinned at Elsie, who was very angry.

'You bad boy, to waste a wish on a thing like that!' she said, and she got up to shake him. She caught hold of his shoulders, and tried to pull him out of the aeroplane.

'I wish you were miles away!' she shouted. 'You're a horrid brother to have!'

The aeroplane's engine started up, and the propeller began to whirl round. Elsie's wish was coming true!

Bobby dragged Elsie in beside him as the aeroplane flew off. 'You horrid girl!' he said. 'That's the second wish gone. Now goodness knows where we shall land.'

They flew in the air for a long way and then the aeroplane landed on a little island. The sea splashed all round it, and except for a few strange trees and sea-birds there was nothing to be seen.

'Now see what you've done!' said Bobby. 'You made us come here!' He got out of the aeroplane

and walked round the little island. He came back looking gloomy.

'We can't stay here. There is nothing to eat. We should starve. We must go back home.'

'How?' said Elsie.

'In the aeroplane,' said Bobby. 'Come on, get in. We'll fly back, and then we'll be very, very careful about what we wish for our last wish.'

They got into the aeroplane – but it didn't fly off. It just stood there, its engine silent and its propeller still.

'I'm afraid we'll have to use our last wish to get back home,' said Bobby, sadly. 'How we have wasted them! Aeroplane, I wish you would take us back home.'

The aeroplane flew up into the air and soon the children were back in the meadow again. They got out and looked at the nice little plane.

'Well, anyway, we've got an aeroplane,' said Bobby. But even as he spoke the little pixie ran up, jumped into the plane, set the engine going, and flew off.

'What did I tell you?' shouted the pixie, leaning out of the aeroplane. 'I said that three wishes would be wasted on children like you – and so they were! People who quarrel always do stupid things – what silly children you are!'

Bobby and Elsie watched the little aeroplane as it flew above the trees. They were very sad.

'If we hadn't quarrelled, we'd have been able to talk over what we really wanted,' said Elsie. 'We could have wished for some lovely things.'

'Well – we will next time,' said Bobby.

But there won't be a next time. Things like that don't happen twice!

It Was The Wind

Tricky and Dob lived next door to one another. Dob was a hard-working little fellow, always busy about something. Tricky was a scamp, and he teased the life out of poor old Dob.

He undid the clothes from Dob's washing-line, so that they dropped into the mud and had to be washed all over again. He crept through a hole in his fence and took the eggs that Feathers, Dob's white hen, laid for him. He borrowed this and he borrowed that – but he always forgot to return anything.

Dob put up with Tricky and his ways very patiently, but he did wish Tricky didn't live next to him!

He didn't like Tricky at all, but he didn't tell tales of him or complain of him, so nobody ever punished Tricky or scolded him.

Still, things can't go on like that for ever, and one day a very funny thing happened.

It was an autumn day, and the leaves had blown down from the trees, spreading everywhere over Dob's garden.

They were making Tricky's garden untidy, too, of course, but he didn't mind a bit. Dob did mind. He was a good little gardener, and he loved his garden to be tidy and neat.

So he took his broom and began to sweep his leaves into a big heap. He swept them up by the fence between his garden and Tricky's. There! Now his garden was tidy again. Dob went to fetch his barrow to put the leaves into it to take down to the rubbish heap.

Tricky had been watching Dob sweeping up his leaves. He grinned. Here was a chance to tease Dob again, he thought. Dob had put the pile of leaves just by the hole in his fence! Tricky slipped out as soon as Dob had gone to fetch his barrow, and went to his fence.

He wriggled through the hole into the middle of the pile of leaves. Then he scattered all the leaves over the grass; what fun he was having. When he had finished, he crept back unseen through the hole.

'Dob *will* be surprised!' he thought. And Dob was. He was annoyed as well. What had happened? A minute ago the leaves had been in a neat pile — now they were all over the place again!

He saw Tricky looking over the fence. 'Good-day, Dob,' said Tricky politely. 'It's a pity the

wind blew your leaves away just as you got them into a pile, wasn't it?'

'The wind?' said Dob, puzzled. 'But there isn't any wind.'

'Well, it must have been a sudden, mischievous breeze, then,' said Tricky, grinning. 'You know – a little young wind that doesn't know any better.'

'Hmm!' said Dob, and he swept up all his leaves into a pile again. It was dinner-time then, so he left them and went indoors. But he did not get his dinner at once. He just watched behind his curtain to see if Tricky came into his garden to kick away his pile of leaves.

Well, he didn't see Tricky, of course, because that mischievous fellow had wriggled through the hole in the fence that was well hidden by the pile of leaves. He was now in the very middle of the pile – and to Dob's enormous surprise his leaves suddenly shot up in the air, and flew all over the grass.

'What a very peculiar thing!' said Dob, astonished. 'I've never seen leaves behave like that before. Can it be that Tricky is right, and that a little breeze is playing about with them?'

He thought about it whilst he ate his dinner. It couldn't be Tricky, because Dob hadn't seen him climb over the fence and go to the pile. One minute the pile had been there, neat and tidy – and the next it had been scattered all over the place.

'I'll sweep up the leaves once more,' thought Dob. 'And I'll put them into my barrow before that wind gets them again.'

But, of course, Tricky got into the next pile too, through the hole in the fence, and Dob found his leaves scattering all round him. He was very cross and very puzzled.

Soon Tricky called to him. He had wriggled out of the pile, through the hole in the fence and was now back in his own garden, grinning away at

Dob. 'My word – are you still sweeping up leaves? There's no end to it, Dob.'

'I think you must have been right when you said that the wind is playing me tricks,' said Dob. 'But the thing is – what am I to do about it?'

'Catch the bad fellow and make him prisoner!' said Tricky.

'But how can you catch the wind?' asked Dob.

'Well, haven't you seen how the wind loves to billow out a sail, or blow out a sack or a balloon?' said Tricky. 'Just get a sack, Dob, put the wind in it when it comes along, tie up the neck and send him off by carrier to the Weather Man to deal with. He'll give him a good telling off, you may be sure!'

'Well – if I *could* catch the wind that way I would certainly do all you say,' said Dob. 'But I'm afraid it isn't possible.'

All the same he went and got a sack and put it ready nearby in case the wind did come along again. Tricky watched him sweep up his leaves once more, and he simply couldn't resist creeping through the hole to play the same trick on poor Dob again!

But this time Dob was on the watch for the wind, and as soon as he saw the leaves beginning to stir, he clapped the sack over the

pile. He felt something wriggling in the leaves, and gave a shout.

'I've got him! I've caught the wind! He's filling up my sack! Aha, you scamp of a wind, I've got you!'

Tricky wriggled and shouted in the sack, but Dob shook him well down to the bottom of it, together with dozens of leaves, and tied up the neck firmly with rope.

'It's no good wriggling and shouting like that!' he said sternly. 'You're caught. It's a good thing Tricky told me how to catch you! Now, off to the Weather Man you're going, and goodness knows what he'll do with you!' He wrote a big label:

'To be delivered to the Weather Man by the Carrier — one small, mischievous breeze. Suggest it should be well spanked before it is allowed to blow again.'

And when the Carrier came by with his cart, Dob handed the whimpering Tricky to him, tightly tied up in the sack. The Carrier read the label and grinned.

'I'll deliver him all right,' he said. 'The Weather Man isn't in a very good temper lately – I'm afraid he'll be very cross with this little breeze.'

Dob went to look over the fence to find Tricky

and tell him that his good idea had been carried out – but Tricky was nowhere to be seen, of course! And he was nowhere to be seen for three whole days! Dob was puzzled.

He came back the evening of the third day. He looked very solemn indeed. The Weather Man had told him off well and truly, and had sent him to do all kinds of blowing errands, which made Tricky very much out of breath.

'Hallo, Tricky! Wherever have you been?' cried Dob.

Tricky wouldn't tell him. He wouldn't tell anyone. But everyone agreed that his three days away had done him good – he wasn't nearly so mischievous, and ever since that day he has never played single trick on old Dob.

'I can't imagine why!' said Dob. How he would laugh if he knew!

The Bed that
Took a Walk

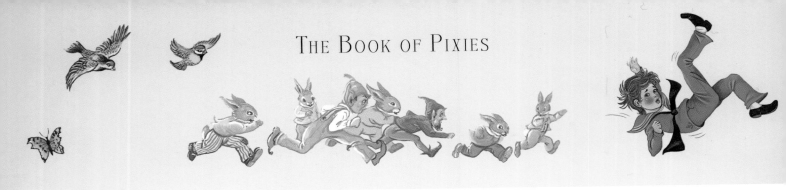

The pixie Miggle was always late for everything. If he went to catch a train he had to run all the way and then he would miss it. If he went to catch a bus it had always gone round the corner before he got there.

'It's just as easy to be early as to be late,' said his friends. 'Why don't you get up a bit sooner, then you would be in time for everything?'

'Well, I'm so sleepy in the mornings,' said Miggle. 'My wife comes and calls me, but I go off to sleep again. I really am a very tired person in the morning.'

'Lazy, he means!' said his friends to one another. 'Never in time for anything! It's shocking. One day he will be very sorry.'

In the month of June the King and Queen of the pixies were coming to visit Apple Tree Town, where Miggle and his friends lived. The pixies were very excited.

'I shall get a new coat,' said Jinky.

'I shall buy a new feather for my hat,' said Twinkle.

'I shall have new red shoes,' said Flitter.

'And I shall buy a whole new suit, a new hat and feathers, and new shoes and buckles with the money I have saved up,' said Miggle. 'I shall be very grand indeed!'

'You'll never be in time to see the King and Queen!' said Jinky, with a laugh.

'Indeed I shall,' said Miggle. 'I shall be up before any of you that day.'

Well, the day before the King and Queen came, Miggle was very busy trying on his new things. The coat didn't quite fit, so he asked his wife to alter it. She stayed up very late trying to make it right.

It was about midnight when Miggle got to bed. How he yawned! 'Wake me up at seven o'clock, wife,' he said. 'Don't forget.'

Mrs. Miggle was tired. 'I shall call you three times, and then, if you don't get up, I shan't call you any more,' she said. ' *I* have to call myself – nobody calls *me* – and I am tired tonight, so I shall not be very patient with you tomorrow if you don't get up when I call you.'

'You *do* sound cross,' said Miggle, and got into bed. He fell fast asleep, and it seemed no time at all before he felt Mrs. Miggle shouting in his ear, and shaking him.

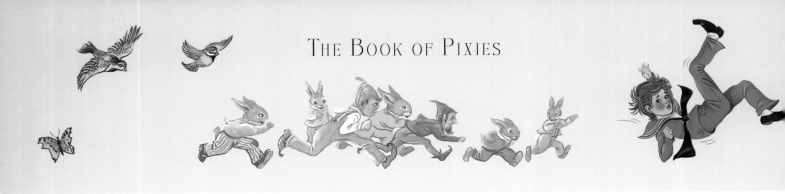

'Miggle! It's seven o'clock. Miggle get up!'

'All right,' said Miggle, and turned over to go to sleep again. In five minutes' time Mrs. Miggle shook him again, and once more he woke up, and went to sleep again.

'This is the third time I've called you,' said Mrs. Miggle, ten minutes later, in a cross voice. 'And it's the last time. If you don't get up now, I shan't call you any more.'

'Right,' said Miggle. 'Just getting up, my dear.' But he didn't. He went to sleep again. Plenty of time to get up and dress and go and see the King and Queen!

Mrs. Miggle kept her word. She didn't call Miggle again. She got dressed in her best frock and went to meet the King and Queen. Miggle slept on soundly, not hearing the footsteps going down the road, as all the pixies hurried by to meet the royal pair.

Miggle's bed creaked to wake him. It shook a little, but Miggle didn't stir. The bed was cross. It thought Miggle stayed too long in it. It knew how upset Miggle would be when he woke up and found that the King and Queen had gone.

So it thought it would take Miggle to the Town Hall, where the King and Queen would be, and perhaps he would wake up there.

The bed walked on its four legs to the door. It squeezed itself through, for it was a narrow bed. It trotted down the street, clickity-clack, clickity-clack.

Miggle didn't wake. He had a lovely dream that he was in a boat that went gently up and down on the sea, and said 'clickity-clack' all the time.

'Gracious! Look, isn't that Miggle asleep on that bed?' cried Jinky, with a squeal of laughter. 'The bed is wide awake, but Miggle isn't – so the bed is taking him to the Town Hall!'

'Clickity-clack, clickity-clack,' went the four legs of the bed. Miggle gave a little snore. He was warm and cosy and comfy, and as fast asleep as ever.

The bed made its way into the Town Hall just as the King and Queen came on to the stage to speak to their people. The pixies jumped to their feet and cheered loudly.

The bed jumped up and down in joy, because it was enjoying the treat too. Miggle woke up when he heard the cheering, and felt the bumping of the bed. He sat up and looked round in the greatest surprise.

'Ha ha, ho ho, look at Miggle,' shouted everyone, and the King and Queen had to smile too. Miggle was full of horror and shame!

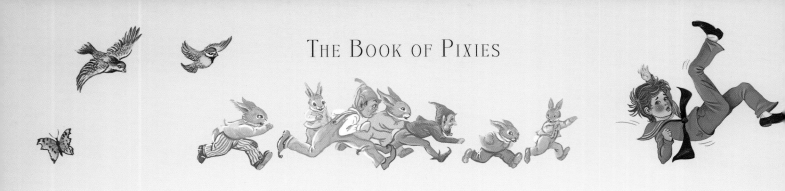

What had happened! Had his silly bed brought him to the Town Hall? Oh dear, and he was in his pyjamas too, instead of in his lovely new clothes!

Miggle could have wept with shame. Mrs. Miggle saw him and went over to him.

'Really, Miggle! To think you've come to see the King and Queen in bed, not even dressed! I'm ashamed of you! What *can* you be thinking of?'

Miggle slid down into bed and pulled the clothes over his head. Mrs. Miggle pulled them off.

'Now you get up and bow properly to His

Majesty the King and Her Majesty the Queen,'
she said.

'What, in my pyjamas?' said poor Miggle.

'Well, if you've come in pyjamas, you'll have to
bow in them,' said Mrs. Miggle. So Miggle had
to stand up on the bed in his pyjamas and bow to
the King and Queen. How they laughed!

'What a funny man!' said the Queen. 'Does he
often do things like this?'

Miggle didn't know what to do. He lay down
again and ordered the bed to go home. But the
bed wasn't a dog, to be ordered here and there. It
wanted to stay and see the fun.

So Miggle had to jump out and run all the
way home in his pyjamas. 'How dreadful, how
dreadful!' he kept thinking, as he ran. 'I can't bear
it! I'd better put on all my fine clothes, and go
back and let the King and Queen see how grand I
really am!'

So he did – but alas, when he got back to the
Town Hall, the King and Queen had just gone.
Everyone was coming away, pleased and excited.
Miggle's bed trotted with them, 'clickity-clack'.

'Hallo, Miggle? Going to ride home asleep in
bed?' cried his friends. 'Oh, how you made the
King and Queen laugh! It was the funniest sight
we've ever seen.'

Miggle frowned and didn't say a word. His bed tried to walk close to him, but he wouldn't let it. Horrid bed! 'I'll never be late again!' thought Miggle. 'Never, never, never!'

But he will. It's not so easy to get out of a bad habit. Won't it be funny if his bed walks off with him again?

The Spell That
Didn't Stop

Old Dame Quick-Eye put her head round the kitchen door, and lazy little Yawner jumped up at once.

'What! Reading again in the middle of the morning before you've done your work!' scolded Dame Quick-Eye. 'Do you want me to put a spell on you and make you grow two more arms and hands? Then you'd have to do twice as much work!'

'Oh no, no,' cried Yawner, shutting his book and beginning to bustle round at once. 'Don't do that.'

'I have three friends coming to dinner,' said Dame Quick-Eye. 'There are all the potatoes and apples to peel and the cabbage to cut up. I shall be very angry if everything isn't ready in time.'

Yawner was very frightened when Dame Quick-Eye was angry. As soon as she had gone he rushed into the kitchen.

'The potatoes! The potatoes! Where are they? And what did I do with those cabbages? Did I fetch them from the garden or didn't I?

Where's the potato knife? Where is it?'

The potato knife was nowhere to be found. Yawner looked everywhere.

'Oh dear, oh dear – the only sharp knife I have! I can't peel the potatoes with a blunt one. I'll never have time to do all this peeling!'

The front door slammed. Yawner saw Dame Quick-Eye going down the path. He stopped rushing about and sat down. He yawned widely. 'Oh dear, what am I to do? I'd better get a spell from the old Dame's room. A spell to peel potatoes and apples! She'll never know.'

He tiptoed upstairs to the strange little room where Dame Quick-Eye did her magic and her spells. There they all were, in boxes and bottles on the shelf. 'Spell for making things Big'. 'Spell for making things Small'. 'Spell for curing a Greedy Person'. 'Spell for growing more Arms and Hands'. 'Spell to cure Yawner of being Lazy'.

'Oh dear,' said Yawner, staring at the bottle with his name on the label. 'I'd better not be lazy any more. Now – where's the spell to Peel Things Quickly?'

'Ah, here it is – good,' he said at last, and picked up a box. In it was a green powder. Yawner hurried downstairs and took up an ordinary knife. He rubbed a little of the green powder on the blade.

'Now peel!' he whispered. 'Peel quickly, quickly. Don't stop!'

He rushed upstairs again and put the little box of powder back on the shelf. Then down he went. Dame Quick-Eye would never know he had taken a bit of her Peeling Spell.

The spell was already working. The knife was hovering over the bowl of potatoes in the sink, and one by one the potatoes rose up to be peeled, falling back with a plop. 'A very pleasant sight to see,' thought Yawner, and he bustled about getting ready the things he needed to lay the table.

The knife peeled all the potatoes in about two minutes. Then it started on the apples. Soon long green parings were scattered all over the draining-board and a dozen apples lay clean and white nearby.

Yawner shot a glance at the busy knife. 'Splendid, splendid! Take a rest, dear knife.'

He rushed into the dining-room to lay the lunch. He rushed back into the kitchen to get the plates – and how he stared! The potato knife was peeling the cold chicken that Yawner had put ready for lunch. It was scraping off long bits of chicken, which fell to the floor and were being eaten by a most surprised and delighted cat.

'Hey!' cried Yawner and rushed at the knife.

'Stop that! You've done your work!'

He tried to catch the knife, but it flew to the dresser and peeled a long strip from that. Then it began to scrape the mantelpiece and big pieces of wood fell into the hearth.

Yawner began to feel frightened. What would Dame Quick-Eye say when she saw all this damage? He rushed at the knife again, but it flew up into the air, darted into the passage and disappeared.

'Well, good riddance to bad rubbish, I say,' said Yawner loudly, and ran to put the potatoes on to boil. He heard Dame Quick-Eye come in with her friends and hurried even more. Lunch mustn't be late!

Then he heard such a to-do in the dining-room and rushed to see what the matter was. What a sight met his eyes!

The potato knife had peeled all the edges of the polished dining-room table. It had peeled every banana, orange, pear and apple in the dishes. It had peeled the backs of all the chairs, and even peeled the top off the clock.

'Look!' cried Dame Quick-Eye in a rage. 'What's been happening? This knife is mad!'

'Bewitched, you mean,' said one of her friends, looking at it closely. 'I can see some green powder

on the blade. Someone's been rubbing it with your Peeling Spell.'

'It's that wretched tiresome lazy little Yawner then!' cried Dame Quick-Eye. 'And there he is — peeping in at the door. Wait till I catch you!'

Yawner didn't wait to hear any more. He ran out into the garden. He kept his broomstick there, and he leapt on it at once.

'Off and away!' he shouted and up in the air rose the broomstick at once.

The broomstick soon became tired of going for miles and miles. It turned itself round and went home again. It sailed down to the yard. Yawner leapt off and rushed to the coal-cellar. He went in and slammed the door. Then he sank down on the coal and cried. Why had he been lazy? Why had he ever stolen a spell? Wrong deeds never, never did any good at all. Dame Quick-Eye looked in at the cellar window. She felt sorry for Yawner.

'Will you be lazy again?' she asked.

'No, Mam,' wept Yawner.

'Will you ever steal my spells again?'

'No, Mam,' said Yawner. 'Never.'

'Then come out and wash up the dirty plates and dishes,' said Dame Quick-Eye, opening the door. 'I've caught the knife and wiped the spell from it. You did a silly and dangerous thing.'

'Yes, Mam,' said Yawner mournfully, and went off to do the dishes.

Dame Quick-Eye hasn't had to use the special 'Spell to cure Yawner of being Lazy'. In fact, she has only to mention spells to make Yawner work twice as hard as usual.

The Three
Bad Imps

There was once three bad imps. They were called Snip, Snap and Snorum, and they really were very naughty. They were very small – not even as tall as a daisy. They had all kinds of jobs to do, and they did them very badly.

They were supposed to help the moths when they crept out of their cocoons – but they pulled them out so roughly that sometimes they spoilt the wings of the little creatures. They had to polish the little coppery beetles that ran through the grasses – and sometimes they polished the beetles' feet too, so that they slipped and slid all over the place!

They were always up to naughty tricks, and nobody could ever catch them to punish them. They were so small, and could hide so easily.

'Nobody will ever catch *me*!' Snip would boast, as he swung up and down on a grass-blade.

'And I can always hide where nobody can find me!' said Snap.

'We're as clever as can be!' said Snorum. And so they were. They got into trouble every day, but

they slipped out of it as easily as worms slip out of their holes!

But one day they really went too far. They had been told to brush the hairs of a furry caterpillar who had fallen into the mud and got very dirty. And instead of brushing his hairs and making him nice and clean again, Snip, Snap and Snorum cut off all his hairs to make themselves little fur coats!

Well, of course, the caterpillar complained very loudly indeed, and the pixies set off to find and catch the three bad imps.

'We'll punish them well!' said the biggest pixie. 'I shall spank each of them with a good, strong grass-blade!'

But nobody could catch those naughty imps. They hid here, and they hid there – and even when they were found, they slipped away easily.

'They have polished themselves all over with the polish they use for the beetles,' said the biggest pixie. 'So, even if we get hold of them, we can't hold them! They slip out of our hands like eels.'

'What shall we do, then?' asked the smallest pixie. 'How can we catch them?'

'Well, first we must find them,' said the biggest pixie. 'Now – where can they be?'

'Send the ants to find out,' said another pixie. 'They can run here, there and everywhere, and they

will soon find where they are hiding.'

So the little brown ants were sent hurrying through the wood, between the grasses, to find the hidden imps. One ant found them and came hurrying back.

'They are asleep in the leaves of the honeysuckle, where it climbs high,' said the tiny ant. 'If you come now, you could catch them.'

'They will slip out of our hands as soon as we touch them,' said the pixies. 'If only we could trap them. Little ant, where could we find a trap that will hold the imps?'

'Only the spiders make traps,' said the ant. 'You might ask *them*.'

So the pixies called the spiders, and they came running over the grass on their eight legs, their eyes looking wisely at the pixies.

'Come with us,' said the pixies. 'We want you to make a trap for some naughty imps.'

So, all together, the pixies and the spiders ran to the honeysuckle, where it climbed high. Softly they all climbed up the twisted stems, and came to where the imps were lying fast asleep among the honeysuckle leaves.

'Can you make a trap to catch them?' whispered the pixies. The spiders looked at one another. Yes – they could!

'There are six of us,' said a fine big spider. 'We can make a cage, if you like – a six-sided cage of web, that will hold the three naughty imps as long as you like!'

'Oh yes!' cried the pixies. 'Make six webs, in the form of a square – four for the sides, one for the top and one for the bottom. That will be a splendid cage. But be careful not to wake the imps.'

The spiders began their work. The pixies watched them. The spiders were very clever indeed. Underneath each spider were little lumps, and from them they drew the thread for their webs.

'These are our spinnerets,' said a big spider to a pixie. 'We spin our web from them. The thread isn't really made till it oozes out of our spinnerets, you know. It squeezes out like a liquid, and the air makes it set, so that we get threads to work with.'

'It's like magic,' said the pixies in wonder. They watched the spiders pull the thread from their spinnerets, more and more and more – as much as they needed.

'Feel the thread,' said a spider. 'It's so fine – and yet so strong.'

'Yes, it is,' said the pixies. 'We would like some to sew our party frocks with! Hurry, spiders, or the imps will wake.'

Each spider chose a leaf, stalk or twig to

hang her outer threads on. It was marvellous to watch them.

After they had fixed their outer threads, they began to make threads that ran to the middle and back, like spokes of a wheel. The three imps slept soundly all the time, for the spiders made no noise at all.

'See how the spiders use their clawed feet to guide the thread,' whispered a pixie. The pixies watched in delight. 'Oh look – now the spiders are running a spiral thread round and round the spokes!'

So they were. They had finished all the spokes, and were now moving round their webs, letting out a thread that went round and round in smaller and smaller circles.

'The imps will never, ever be able to escape from this trap,' said a pixie.

'We will make the web sticky too,' said a spider. 'If we hang tiny sticky drops along the threads, the imps will find themselves caught fast if they try to break through!'

'I have seen flies caught in webs,' said a pixie. 'I suppose the stickiness holds them fast, spider?'

'Of course,' said the spider, pulling a thread tighter. 'Now – we have finished. Shall we go and hide under leaves, and watch what happens?'

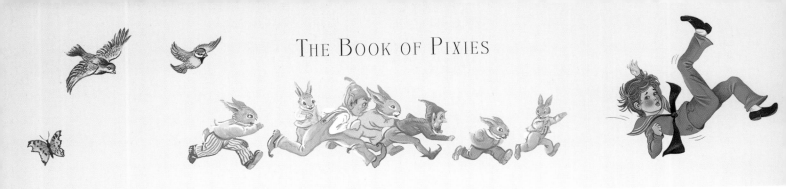

'Yes,' said the pixies. So the spiders ran up to some leaves, and hid themselves there, waiting silently, just as they did when they waited for flies to come.

Soon the imps awoke and stretched themselves – and they saw the trap they were in! They jumped to their feet in alarm.

'What's this! We're in a cage!'

'It's a cage made of spider's web!'

'Break it, break it!'

The three imps flung themselves against the webby walls of the strange cage. They broke the threads – but in a trice the sticky web fell on their arms and legs and heads – and they were caught!

They struggled, and they wriggled, but it was no use. The strong, sticky threads held them as tightly as they could hold flies. Down rushed the spiders and, pouring out more thread from their spinnerets, they rolled the imps round and round in it, until they were helpless.

'Thank you, spiders,' said the pixies. 'We are very grateful to you. Now at last we have caught these bad little imps! They will be well punished!'

'If you want our help again at any time, just let us know,' said the spiders. 'We'll come running to you on our eight long legs!'

The imps were carried off by the pixies – and

dear me, didn't they get a telling off! They sobbed and they cried, and they promised they would be as good as gold.

And so far, they have – you'll find that the caterpillars have their hairs well brushed, and the ladybirds and beetles are well polished now.

But the imps keep away from the spiders. They have never forgotten how they were caught in a webby trap, spun by the six clever spiders!

Silky and
the Snail

Silky was a pixie. She lived under a hawthorn hedge, and often talked to the birds and animals that passed by her house.

One day a big snail came crawling slowly by. Silky had never seen a snail, and at first she was quite afraid. Then she ran up to the snail, and touched his hard shell.

'How clever you are!' she said. 'You carry your house about with you! Why do you do that?'

'Well, you see,' said the snail, 'I have a very soft body that many birds and other creatures like to eat – so I grow a shell to protect it.'

'What a good idea,' said the pixie. 'Can you put your body right inside your shell, snail?'

'Watch me!' said the snail, and he curled his soft body up quickly into his shell. There was nothing of him to be seen except his spiral shell.

'Very clever,' said the pixie. 'Come out again, please, snail. I want to talk to you.'

The snail put his head out and then more of his body. He had four feelers on his head, and the pixie looked at them.

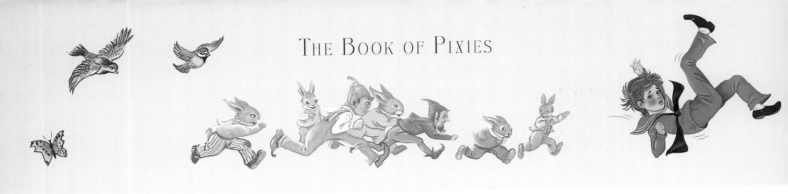

'Haven't you any eyes?' she said. 'I can't see your eyes, snail.'

'Oh, I keep them at the top of my longer pair of feelers,' said the snail. 'Can't you see them? Right at the top, pixie – little black things.'

'Oh yes, I can see them now,' said the pixie. 'What a funny place to keep your eyes, snail! Why do you keep them there?'

'Well, it's rather nice to have my eyes high up on feelers I can move about here and there,' said the snail. 'Wouldn't *you* like eyes on the ends of movable feelers, pixie? Think what a lot you could see!'

'I should be afraid that they would get hurt, if I had them at the end of feelers,' said Silky.

'Oh no!' said the snail, and he did such a funny thing. He rolled his eyes down inside his feelers, and the pixie stared in surprise.

'Oh, you can roll your eyes down your feelers, just as I pull the toe of my stocking inside out!' she said. 'Sometimes I put my hand inside my stocking, catch hold of the toe, and pull it down inside the stocking, to turn it inside out – and you do the same with your eyes!'

'Yes, I do,' said the snail. 'It's rather a good idea, don't you think so?'

'Oh, *very* good,' said Silky. 'Where's your

mouth? Is that it, under your feelers?'

'Yes,' said the snail, and he opened it to show the pixie. She looked at it closely.

'Have you any teeth?' she said. 'I have a lot.'

'So have I,' said the snail. 'I have about fourteen thousand.'

Silky stared. 'You shouldn't tell silly stories like that,' she said.

'I'm not telling silly stories,' said the snail. 'I'll show you my teeth.'

He put out a long, narrow tongue, and Silky laughed. 'Don't tell me that you grow teeth on your *tongue*,' she said.

'Well, I do,' said the snail. 'Just look at my tongue, pixie. Can't you see the tiny teeth there, hundreds and hundreds of them?'

'Oh *yes*,' said the pixie in surprise. 'I can. They are so tiny, snail, and they all point backwards. It's like a tooth-ribbon, your tongue. How do you eat with your teeth?'

'I use my tongue like a file,' said the snail. 'I'll show you.'

He went to a lettuce, put out his tongue, and began to rasp away at a leaf. In a moment he had eaten quite a big piece.

'Well, you really are a strange creature,' said Silky. She looked closely at the snail, and noticed

a strange little hole opening and shutting in the top of his neck.

'What's that slit for, in your neck?' she asked. 'And why does it keep opening and shutting?'

'Oh, that's my breathing-hole,' said the snail. 'Didn't you guess that? Every time that hole opens and shuts, I breathe.'

'Why don't you breathe with your mouth, as I do?' asked Silky.

'All soft-bodied creatures like myself, that have no bones at all, breathe through our bodies,' said the snail. 'Now, if you will excuse me, I must get into my shell. I can see the big thrush coming.'

He put his body back into his shell and stayed quite still. The thrush passed by without noticing him. The pixie went into her house, and came out with a tin of polish and a duster.

'Snail, I am going to polish up your shell for you,' she said. 'I shall make you look so nice. Everyone will say how beautiful you are!'

'Oh, thank you,' said the snail, and he stayed quite still whilst Silky put polish on her cloth and then rubbed his shell hard.

'I rather like that,' he said.

'Well, come every day and I'll give you a good rubbing with my duster,' promised the pixie.

So, very soon, the two became good friends, and

the snail always came by the pixie's house for a chat whenever he was near.

One day Silky was sad. She showed the snail a necklace of bright-blue beads – but it was broken, for the clasp was lost.

'I wanted to wear this at a party tomorrow,' said Silky. 'But I can't get anyone to mend it for me.'

'I know someone who will,' said the snail. 'He is a great friend of mine. He lives in a tiny house the fifth stone to the left of the old stone wall, and the fifteenth up. There's a hole there, and Mendy lives in it, doing all kinds of jobs for everyone.'

'I would never find the way,' said Silky. 'I know I'd get lost.'

'Well, I will take the necklace for you tonight,' said the snail. 'But I know Mendy will take a little time to do it, so you would have to fetch it yourself some time tomorrow.'

'But I should get lost!' said Silky.

'I will see that you don't,' said the snail. 'I will take the necklace to Mendy, give it to him, and come straight back here. And behind me I will leave a silvery trail for you to follow!'

'Oh, snail, you are kind and clever!' said Silky, delighted. She hung the beads over the snail's feelers, and he set off towards the old wall he knew

so well. It was a long way for him to go, because he travelled very slowly.

It was a dry evening and the soft body of the snail did not get along as easily as on a wet night. So he sent out some slime to help his body along, and then he glided forwards more easily.

The slimy trail dried behind him, and left a beautiful silvery path, easy to see. The snail went up the wall to the hole where old Mendy the brownie lived, and gave him the broken necklace.

'It will be ready at noon tomorrow,' said Mendy. 'Thank you,' said the snail, and went home again, very slowly, leaving behind him a second silvery trail, running by the first.

Silky was asleep, so he didn't wake her, but he told her next morning that her necklace would be ready at noon.

'And you can't get lost,' he said, 'because I have left two silvery paths for you to follow. It doesn't matter which you walk on – either of them will lead you to Mendy.'

So Silky set off on one of the silvery paths, and it led her to the old wall, up it, and into Mendy's little house. Her necklace was mended, so she put it on ready for the party. She was very pleased indeed.

'Thank you,' she said. 'Now I know the way to

your house, I'll bring some other things for you to mend, Mendy!'

She went to find her friend, the snail. 'Thank you for leaving me such a lovely silvery path,' she said. 'I do think you are clever!'

I expect you would like to see the snail's silvery path too, wouldn't you? Well, go round your garden any summer's morning – you are sure to see the snail's night-time trail of silver gleaming in the sunshine here and there.

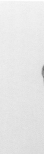

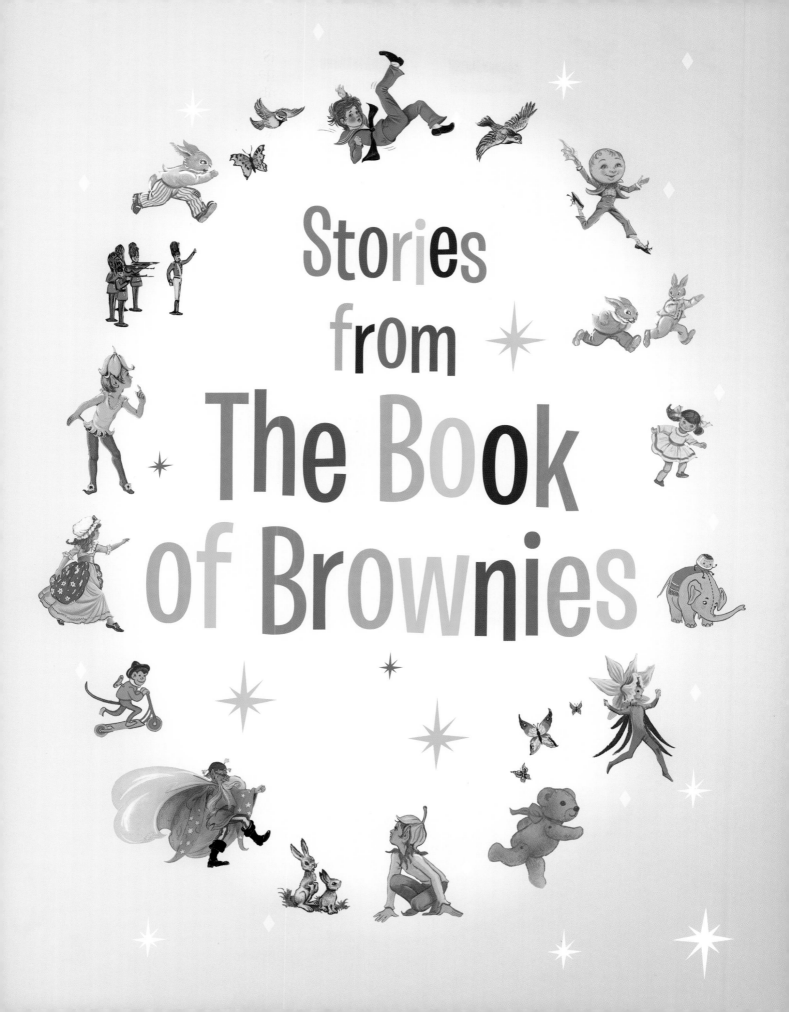

Stories from The Book of Brownies

Hop Skip and Jump Play a Naughty Trick

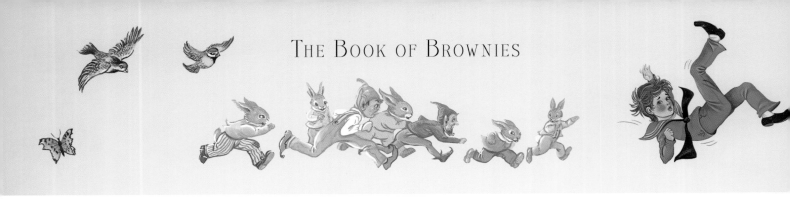

Hop, Skip and Jump were just finishing their breakfast one morning when they heard the postman rat-tatting on all the knockers down the street.

'Dear me!' said Hop. 'Everybody seems to be getting a letter this morning! Perhaps we shall too.'

The three brownies leaned out of the window of Crab-apple Cottage and watched the postman come nearer. Next door but one, rat-tat! And a large letter fell into the letter-box. Next door, rat-tat! Another large letter, just like the first.

'I wonder whatever the letters are!' said Skip. 'They're all the same and everyone is having one, so there'll be one for us too!'

But there wasn't. The postman walked right past Crab-apple Cottage.

'Hey!' called Jump. 'You've missed us out! Come back, postman!'

The postman shook his head.

'There isn't a letter for you,' he said, and rat-

tatted on the knocker of the cottage next door.

Well, Hop, Skip and Jump *were* upset. No letter for them, when everyone else had one! Whoever could be writing letters and missing them out!

'Let's go and ask Gobo next door what his letter's about,' said Hop.

So the three brownies hopped into Gobo's. They found him looking very pleased and excited, reading his letter out loud to Pinkie, his wife.

'What's it all about?' asked Skip.

'Listen! Just listen!' said Gobo. 'It's an invitation from the King. This is what he says: "His Majesty, the King of Fairyland, is giving a Grand Party on Thursday. Please come".'

'Oh!' cried the brownies. 'Then why haven't *we* been asked?'

Gobo looked surprised.

'Haven't you had a letter?' he asked. 'Oh well, there must be a reason for it. Have you been good lately?'

'Not *very*,' said Hop.

'Not *much*, said Skip.

'Not at all,' said Jump, who was the most truthful of the three.

'Well, there you are,' said Gobo, folding up his letter. 'You know the King never asks bad

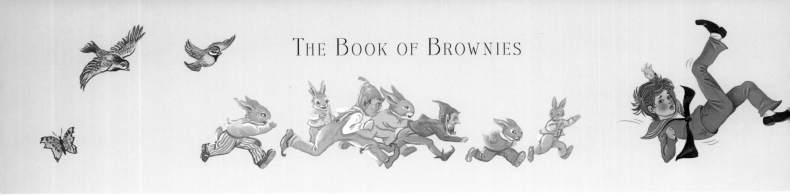

brownies to his parties. You can't expect to be invited if you *will* be naughty.'

The brownies went out crossly. They ran back into Crab-apple Cottage and sat down round the table.

'What have we done that was naughty lately?' asked Hop.

'We painted Old Mother Wimple's pig green,' said Skip.

'Yes, and we got on to Gillie Brownie's cottage roof and put fireworks down her chimney,' said Jump.

'And we put a bit of prickly gorse in that horrid old Wizard's bed,' said Hop. 'Oh dear – perhaps we *have* been a bit naughtier than usual.'

'And someone's told the King,' sighed Skip.

'So we've been left out of the party,' groaned Jump. 'Well, it serves us right!'

Everybody except the three bad brownies had got an invitation. Brownie Town was most excited.

'It's going to be a *very* grand party!' said Gobo next door, who was busy making himself a new suit. 'There's going to be dancing and conjuring, and presents for everybody!'

This made Hop, Skip and Jump feel more disappointed than ever.

'Can't we go somehow?' wondered Hop. 'Can't

we dress up and pretend to be someone else, not ourselves?'

'We haven't got a card to show,' said Skip mournfully.

'Look, there's Gobo's wife,' said Jump, pointing through the window. 'What's she looking upset about? Hey, Pinkie, what's the matter?'

'Oh, a *great* disappointment,' answered Pinkie. 'The conjurer that the King was going to have at the party can't come after all, and the Lord High Chamberlain can't get anyone else. *Isn't* it disappointing?'

'Not so disappointing for us as for you!' said Hop. Then a great idea came to him, and he turned to Skip and Jump.

'I say!' he said, with his naughty little eyes twinkling. 'I say, couldn't we pretend we were conjurers and get the Lord High Chamberlain to let us in to the party?'

'What a fine idea!' cried Skip and Jump in delight. 'You can be the conjurer, Hop, and we'll be your assistants!'

'But what tricks shall we do?' asked Hop. 'We don't know how to do any yet!'

All that morning the brownies tried to think of conjuring tricks to do at the party, but although they tried their hardest to make rabbits come out

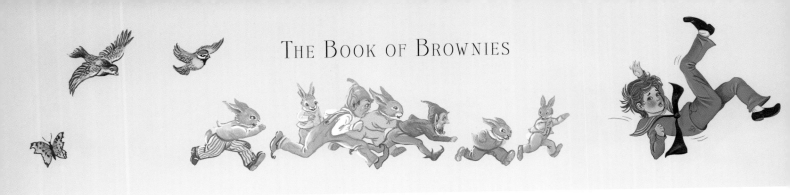

of hats, and ribbons come out of their mouths, it wasn't a bit of good, they just couldn't do it.

They were having dinner, and feeling very unhappy about everything, when a knock came at the door.

'Come in!' cried Hop.

The door opened and an old woman with green eyes looked in.

'Good afternoon,' she said, 'do you want to buy any magic?'

'She's a witch!' whispered Jump. 'Be careful of her.'

'What sort of magic?' asked Hop.

'Oh, any sort,' said the witch, coming into the room. 'Look here!'

She took Hop's watch, rubbed it between her hands, blew on it, and opened her hands again. The watch was gone!

'Buttons and buttercups!' gasped Hop in astonishment. 'Where's it gone to?'

'You'll find it in the teapot,' said the witch.

Skip lifted the lid of the teapot, and there, sure enough, lay the watch, half covered in tea-leaves. He fished it out with a spoon. Hop was very cross.

'I call that a *silly* trick!' he said. 'Why, you might have spoilt my watch!'

'Do something else, Miss Witch,' begged Jump.

'Give me your tea-cup,' said the witch.

Jump gave it to her. The witch filled it full of tea, covered it with a plate, whistled on the plate, and took it off again.

'Oh,' cried Jump, hardly believing his eyes, 'it's full of little goldfish!'

So it was – the tiniest, prettiest little things you ever saw! The brownies thought it was wonderful.

Then the witch emptied Jump's tea into Skip's cup. And, hey presto! all the fishes vanished.

The brownies began to feel as if they were dreaming.

'If only we could do one or two tricks like that!' sighed Hop. 'Why, we could get into the King's party as easily as anything.'

'Oho, so you want to go to the party, do you?' asked the witch. 'Haven't you been invited?'

'No,' answered Skip, and he told the witch all about it. She listened hard.

'Dear, dear!' she said at the end. 'It really is a shame not to invite nice little brownies like you! Listen – if I get you into the Palace as conjurers, will you do the trick I want you to? It's a very, very special one.'

'Show us it!' said the brownies, beginning to feel most excited.

The witch went outside and came back carrying

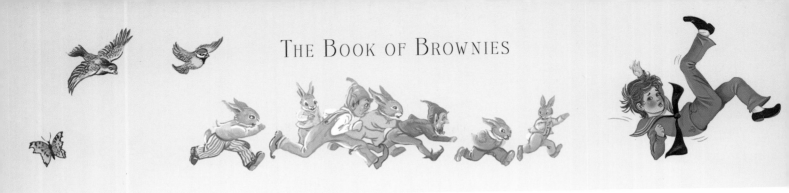

a round green basket, with a yellow lid. She put it on the floor.

'Now you,' she said, pointing to Hop, 'jump into this basket!'

Hop jumped inside. The witch put the lid on. Then she tapped three times on the top of it and sang:

'Rimminy, romminy ray
My magic will send you away;
Rimminy, romminy ro
Ever so far you will go!'

Skip and Jump looked at the basket. It didn't move or creak!

'Take off the lid and look inside,' said the witch.

Skip took off the lid and almost fell into the basket in surprise. 'Oh!' he shouted. 'Oh! Hop's gone, and the basket's empty.'

So it was. There was nothing in it at all.

'Now watch,' said the witch, and putting the lid on again, she began singing:

'Rimminy, romminy ray
Hear the spell and obey;
Rimminy, romminy relf
Jump out of the basket yourself!'

Immediately, the lid flew off and out jumped Hop, looking as pleased as could be.

'Good gracious!' gasped Jump, sitting down suddenly on a chair. 'Where have you been, Hop?'

'In the basket all the time,' said Hop.

'But you *weren't*, we looked!' said Skip.

'You couldn't have,' said Hop, 'or you'd have seen me!'

'We *did* look, I tell you,' said Skip crossly.

'Be quiet,' said the witch. 'It's the magic in the basket that does the trick. Now listen – I'll lend you that basket if you'll promise to do the trick at the party in front of the King and Queen.'

'Of course we will, of course we will!' cried the brownies. 'But why do you lend it to us for nothing?'

'Oh, just because I'm kind-hearted,' said the witch, grinning very wide indeed. 'But mind – when you've got into the basket and have vanished, and been brought back, you've got to offer to do the same thing with anyone else. Perhaps the King will offer to get into the basket, or the Queen, or the Princess!'

'My!' said Hop, 'do you think they will?'

'They're almost sure to,' said the witch. 'So mind you let them try. But you must remember this. If any of the Royal Family get in, tap seven

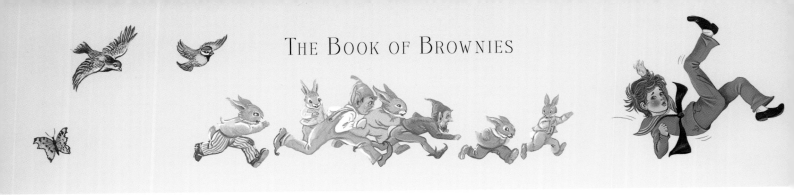

times, not three times, on the lid when you sing
the magic verse. Three times for ordinary folk, but
seven times for royalty – see?'

'Yes, we'll remember,' promised Skip, 'and
thank you very much for lending us such a
lovely trick.'

When the witch had gone, leaving behind her
the green basket with its yellow lid, the three
brownies were tremendously excited. They began
to plan their clothes for the next day, and spent all
the afternoon and evening making them.

Hop looked very grand in a black velvet suit
with a long red cloak and peaked hat. Skip and
Jump were dressed like pages and were just alike
in bright green suits.

When the party day came they all went out very
early with the magic basket and hid in a nearby
wood, for they didn't want any of the brownies to
see them and guess what they were going to do.

'I hope they have lots of lovely things for tea,'
said Hop. 'I'm getting very hungry.'

'It will soon be time to go,' said Skip. 'Listen!
There are the drums to say that the first guests
have arrived!'

'Come along then,' said Jump. 'We'll arrive too!'

'Now remember, I'm Twirly-wirly the Great
Conjurer from the Land of Tiddlywinks,' said

Hop, 'and you are my two assistants. Don't forget you've got to be polite to me and bow each time you speak to me!'

Off they went, all feeling a little nervous. But Hop, who was bigger than the others and rather fat, looked so grand in his red cloak, that Skip and Jump soon began to feel nobody could possibly guess their secret.

At last they reached the Palace Gates.

'Your cards,' said the sentry to Hop, Skip, and Jump.

'I am Twirly-wirly, the Great Conjurer from the Land of Tiddlywinks,' said Hop, in such a grand voice that Skip and Jump wanted to laugh. 'I am here to take the place of the conjurer who could not come.'

The sentry let them pass.

'Go straight up the drive,' he said, 'and at the top of the first flight of steps you will find the Lord High Chamberlain.'

The three brownies went on. Hop was enjoying himself. He told the others to walk behind him and bow to him, whenever they saw him turn their way.

'You're getting a great deal too grand,' grumbled Jump, who began to wish he was the conjurer instead of Hop, for he was carrying

the basket and finding it rather heavy.

The Lord High Chamberlain was very surprised to see them. He was even more surprised when he heard Hop telling him who he was.

'Twirly-wirly, the Great Conjurer,' he said, pretending to know all about him. 'Dear me, what an honour to be sure! Very kind of you to have come, *very* kind. Pray come this way!'

He led them to a tea table and gave Hop a chair. Skip and Jump stood behind him, and looked longingly at the cakes and jellies, tarts and custards spread out on the table in front of Hop.

Little pages ran up and offered all the nicest things to the conjurer. He took some of each, and Skip and Jump looked on enviously.

'Aren't *we* going to have any?' whispered Skip in Hop's ear. 'You're not going to leave us out, are you?'

'Hush!' said Hop. 'You are only my servants today. If you don't keep quiet I shall keep turning round to you and you'll have to bow till your backs ache!'

Hop had an enormous tea. Then he announced to the Lord High Chamberlain that he would now come and do his famous trick with his magic basket, if Their Majesties the King and Queen would like to see it.

Their Majesties at once sent a message to say they would be very pleased to see it.

'Come this way,' said the Chamberlain, and led the three brownies to where the King and Queen sat on their thrones. In front of them was a square piece of grass, and round it sat scores of fairies and gnomes, brownies and elves, all waiting to see Twirly-wirly the Great Conjurer.

Hop stepped grandly up to the King and Queen, and bowed three times. So did Skip and Jump.

'I will now do my wonderful basket trick' said Hop in a very loud and haughty voice. Then he turned to Skip.

'Bring me the basket,' he ordered. Skip rushed forward with it in such a hurry that he tumbled over, and everyone began laughing. Jump helped him up, and together they picked up the magic basket.

'Get into it,' commanded Hop, pointing at Skip. Skip jumped in.

'Put the lid on!' Hop commanded Jump. Jump did so. Then Hop tapped three times on the lid and sang:

> 'Rimminy, romminy ray
> My magic will send you away;

Rimminy, romminy ro
Ever so far you will go!'

Everybody listened and watched, and wondered what was going to happen. The King and Queen bent forward to get a better view, and the little Princess Peronel stood up in her excitement.

'Take the lid off!' ordered Hop.

Jump took the lid off. The basket was empty!

'Ooh!' said everyone in the greatest surprise. 'Ooh! He's gone!'

'Roll the basket round for everyone to see that it's empty,' commanded Hop, who was now thoroughly enjoying himself.

Jump rolled the basket round so that everyone could have a good look. Then he brought it back to Hop.

'Put the lid on!' said Hop. Jump put it on. Everybody stopped breathing, to see whatever was going to happen next.

Hop tapped three times on the lid and sang the magic song:

'Rimminy, romminy ray
Hear the spell and obey;
Rimminy, romminy relf,
Jump out of the basket yourself!'

Just as he finished, the lid flew off and out jumped Skip in his little green suit, looking as perky as anything! He capered about and bowed to everyone.

'Oh look! Oh look! He's come back again!' shouted the fairies and brownies. 'Oh, what a wonderful trick! Do it again, do it again!'

Hop bowed very low. 'Would anyone care to come and get into the basket?' he asked. 'I will do the trick with anyone.'

'Oh let *me*, let *me*!' cried a little silvery voice, and who should come running on the grass but the Princess Peronel!

'Come back, Peronel!' cried the King. 'You're not to get into that basket!'

'Oh please, oh, please,' she begged. 'It's my birthday and you *said* I could have anything I wanted.'

'No, no!' said the Queen. 'You mustn't get into that basket! Come back!'

'I shall cry then!' said Peronel, screwing up her pretty little face.

'Oh dear, oh dear!' said the King, who couldn't bear to see Peronel cry.

'You'd better have your own way then, but make haste about it!'

Peronel jumped into the green basket, and Skip

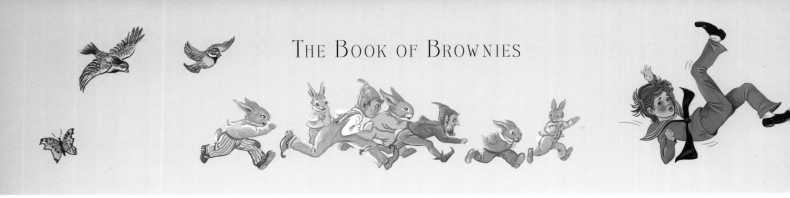

clapped on the lid. Hop remembered what the witch had told him – he must tap the lid seven times for royalty. So, very solemnly, he did so. Then he and Skip and Jump all chanted the magic rhyme together.

'Rimminy, romminy ray
My magic will send you away;
Rimminy, romminy ro
Ever so far you will go!'

But, oh dear, oh dear, oh dear! Whatever *do* you think happened?

Why, just as the magic rhyme was finished, the basket rose into the air, and sailed right away! Higher and higher it went, over the trees and over the palace, towards the setting sun.

'Oh! Oh!' cried the Queen, jumping up in terrible distress. 'Where's my Peronel gone to? Bring her back, quickly!'

But Hop, Skip and Jump were just as surprised as anyone! What an extraordinary thing for the basket to do!

'Arrest those conjurers!' suddenly said the King, in an awful voice.

Six soldiers at once ran up and clapped their hands on the brownies' shoulders.

'Now, unless you bring Peronel back *at once*,' said the King, 'you go straight to prison, and I'll have your heads cut off in the morning!'

'Oh, no, no!' cried the brownies, very frightened indeed. 'Please, please, we aren't conjurers! Only just brownies!'

'Nonsense!' stormed the King. 'Ordinary brownies can't do tricks like that! Now then, are you going to bring Peronel back again?'

'I can't, I can't,' wailed Hop, big tears beginning to pour down his cheeks. 'I'm only a naughty brownie dressed up like a conjurer, because you didn't ask me to your party!'

Suddenly a watching brownie gave a shout of surprise. It was Gobo. He ran up to Hop and pulled off his peaked hat and red cloak.

'Why, it's Hop!' he cried, in astonishment. 'Your Majesty, these brownies are Hop, Skip and Jump, the three naughty brownies of our town.'

'Goodness gracious!' said the King, in a terribly upset voice. 'This is more serious than I thought. If they are really brownies, then they cannot bring back Peronel. But where did you get the basket from?' he asked Hop sternly.

Hop dried his eyes and told the King all about the witch's visit, and how she had left the basket with them.

'Oh, it's Witch Green-eyes!' groaned the King. 'She's often vowed to steal Peronel away and now she's done it through you, you naughty, stupid little brownies.'

'My goodness!' said Hop. 'Do you think the witch has *really* stolen her for always?'

'Yes!' sobbed the Queen, who was terribly distressed. 'We shall never get her back again, the darling!'

'Oh my goodness!' said Skip, in a frightened voice.

'Oh my goodness!' wailed Jump, in a miserable voice.

'Oh your goodness!' roared the King suddenly, in a temper. 'What do you mean, oh your *goodness*! You ought to say, "Oh your badness," you mischievous little brownies! You haven't a bit of goodness among the three of you. And now see what you've done! I've a good mind to cut off your heads!'

'Oh my goodness!' wept Hop again. He didn't mean to say it, but he couldn't think of anything else.

The King grew angrier than ever.

'Where *is* your goodness?' he demanded.

'Yes, where *is* it?' shouted everybody.

'We d-d-don't know,' stammered the brownies in dismay.

'Well, go and find it!' stormed the King. 'Go

along! Go right out of Fairyland, and don't come back till you've found your goodness that you keep talking about! Make haste before I cut off your heads!'

'Oh, oh, oh!' cried the three brownies in a great fright, and they all took to their heels and fled. Down the steps they went and down the drive, and out through the palace gates past the astonished sentries.

Even then they didn't stop. They rushed down the road and into the Cuckoo Wood, as if a thousand soldiers were after them!

At last, out of breath, tired and unhappy, they sat down under a big oak tree.

'Oh my goodness!' began Hop.

'Don't be silly!' said Skip. '*Don't* keep saying that. We're in a terrible, terrible fix.'

'To be turned out of Fairyland!' wept Jump. 'Oh, what a terrible punishment! And how can we find our goodness? Of course we never shall! People don't have goodness they can find!'

'It's just the King's way of banishing us from Fairyland altogether,' wept Hop. 'He knows we'll never be able to go back. And, oh dear, whatever's happened to poor little Peronel?'

What indeed? None of the brownies knew, and they were very unhappy.

'The only thing to do now is to go and see if we can find Peronel and rescue her,' said Jump. 'We'll sleep here for the night, and start off in the morning, on our way to Witchland.'

So all night long they slept beneath the big oak tree, and dreamed of horrid magic baskets, and packets of goodness that would keep running away from them.

Their Adventure in the Cottage Without a Door

Next morning the brownies set out on their journey. They soon passed the borders of Fairyland and found themselves in the Lands Outside. For a long, long time they walked, and met nobody at all.

'I *am* getting hungry!' sighed Hop.

'So am I!' said Skip.

'Well, look! There's a cottage,' said Jump. 'We'll go and ask if we can have something to eat. Have you got any money, Hop?'

Hop felt in his pockets.

'Not a penny,' he answered.

'Oh dear, nor have I,' said Skip.

'What *are* we to do then?' asked Jump. 'Perhaps there's someone kind living in the cottage, who will give us some breakfast for nothing.'

The three brownies went up to the little cottage. It was surrounded by trees and its front door was painted a very beautiful bright blue.

Hop knocked loudly.

'Who is knocking at my door?' asked a deep voice.

'Three hungry brownies,' answered Hop boldly.

'Come in!' said the voice.

Hop opened the door and the brownies went in.

Clap! The door swung to behind them, and made them jump. Hop looked round to see who had shut the door.

But to his enormous surprise, he could see no door at all – and yet they had just come in by one.

'Good gracious!' he cried. 'Wherever has the door gone!'

'He, he!' chuckled a deep voice. 'It's gone where *you* won't find it! I've got you prisoners now. Three nice little servants to work for me all day!'

Hop, Skip and Jump looked most astonished. This was a fine sort of welcome!

Then they saw an old wizard, huddled up by the cottage fire, laughing at them.

'We're not your prisoners, so please let us go,' said Hop.

'All right, go!' laughed the wizard.

But search as they would, the brownies couldn't find any door at all. There were blank walls all round them. Then they knew that they were prisoners indeed.

'Now, listen,' said the wizard. 'I will give you your meals, and in return you must work for me. I have a great many spells I want copied out. Sit

down at that table and begin work at once.'

The three brownies obeyed. They knew that it was best not to anger such a powerful wizard.

He brought them each a great book of magic, and set it down beside them.

'Begin at page one,' he said, 'and if you make me a fair copy of all the books, without one single mistake, perhaps I will let you go.'

'Oh dear!' groaned Jump. 'Why, the books have got about a thousand pages each.'

The three brownies set to work, and very difficult it was too, for the wizard wrote so badly that they could hardly read his writing in the big magic books.

All day they wrote, and all the wizard gave them to eat was a large turnip, which tasted just like India-rubber. The brownies kept looking round to see if the door came back again, but alas, it didn't.

That night, when the wizard was snoring on his bed, the three brownies began whispering together.

'We *must* escape somehow!' said Hop.

'But how?' whispered Skip and Jump.

None of them could think of a plan at all.

'It's no good thinking of escaping until we find out about that disappearing door!' groaned Hop.

'The wizard's barred the window right across. We'd better go to sleep.'

So off to sleep they went, and were wakened up very early the next morning by the wizard, who wanted his breakfast.

After that they had to sit down and copy out the magic books again. It was dreadfully dull work.

But suddenly Hop found he was copying out something that made his heart beat with excitement. It was about Disappearing Doors.

'A Disappearing Door will come back if a wizard's green stick is swung three times in the air and dropped,' said the book. Hop's hand shook as he copied it out.

'If only the wizard's stick is green, and I could get hold of it whilst he's asleep!' he thought.

He turned round to look at the stick. Yes, it was green, sure enough – but the wizard was holding it tightly in his hand.

'But when he's asleep, he'll put it down!' thought Hop, longing to tell Skip and Jump what he had discovered.

That night he watched the wizard carefully – but oh, how disappointed he was to see that he went to bed with his stick still held in his hand.

'I'd be sure to wake him if I tried to get his stick!' thought Hop, and he whispered to Skip and

Jump all that he had thought of during the day.

They were most excited. 'Oh, do let's try to get his stick!' whispered Skip. 'If only we could get out of this horrid cottage!'

'And if only we could go back to dear old Fairyland!' whispered Jump, with tears in his eyes.

Now Hop was the bravest of the brownies, and he couldn't bear to see Jump crying.

'I'll go and see if I can possibly get the stick!' he said. 'Stay here and don't make a sound.'

Then the brave little brownie crept quietly across the floor till he reached the wizard's bed.

'Snore – snore!' went the wizard. 'Snore – snore!'

Carefully, Hop put up his hand and felt in the bedclothes for the green stick. But oh my! No sooner did he catch hold of it, than what do you think happened?

Why, that stick jumped straight out of bed by itself and began to chase Hop all round the room. Poor Hop began to yell in fright. That woke the wizard up. He sat up in bed and chuckled.

'He, he,' he laughed, 'so you were trying to steal my stick, were you! Well, well! You won't do it again in a hurry!'

Poor Hop was running all over the place trying to get out of the way of the stick, which gave him the biggest chase he'd ever had in his life.

'Come back, stick!' at last said the wizard, and the stick jumped back into bed with him. Hop ran over to the others.

'This all comes of our last naughty trick at the King's Palace,' he sobbed. 'If only we could go back to Brownie Town, I'd never be bad again!'

After that the brownies knew it was no good trying to get the stick away from the wizard. They were much too afraid of it.

'We must think of something else,' sighed Skip.

Each night the brownies whispered together, but they couldn't think of any plans at all. Then one day the wizard had a visitor.

He was a red goblin, and the ugliest little fellow you could think of. He didn't come in by the vanished door, nor by the window, so the brownies thought he must have jumped down the chimney.

'Good morning,' he said to the wizard. 'Have you those spells you were going to give me?'

'They are not ready yet,' answered the wizard, so humbly and politely that the brownies pricked up their ears.

'Oh, ho,' they thought, 'this red goblin must be someone more powerful than the wizard, for the wizard seems quite frightened of him!'

'Not ready!' growled the goblin. 'Well, see that they are ready by tomorrow, or I'll spirit you away

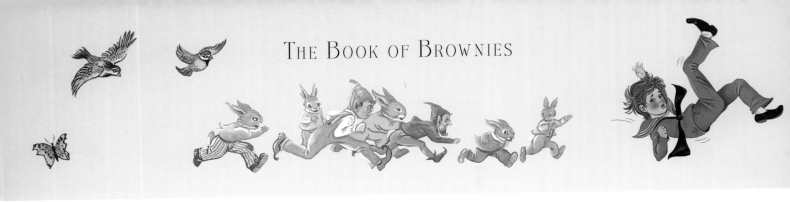

to the highest mountain in the world.'

The wizard shivered and shook, and told the goblin he would be sure to have the spells ready by the next day.

'Mind you do,' said the goblin, and jumped straight up the chimney.

The brownies stared open-mouthed. Then Hop had a wonderful idea. He turned to the wizard.

'That goblin is much more clever than you, isn't he?' he said.

'Pooh!' growled the wizard, angrily. 'I can do things he can't do.'

'Can you really?' asked Hop, opening his eyes very wide. 'What can you do?'

'Well, I can make myself as big as a giant!' said the wizard.

'That's a wonderful thing,' said Hop. 'Let's see you do it!'

'Yes, let's,' said Skip and Jump, seeing that Hop was following out an idea he had suddenly thought of.

The wizard muttered a few words, and rubbed his forehead with some ointment out of a purple box. All at once he began to grow enormously big. Bump! His head touched the ceiling, so the wizard sat down on the floor. Still he went on growing, until once again his head touched the ceiling, and

he filled the cottage from wall to wall. The three brownies had to jump on the window-sill to get out of his way.

'Wonderful! Wonderful!' cried Hop, clapping his hands. 'You're a giant now!'

The wizard looked pleased. He muttered something else and quickly grew smaller, till he reached his own size again.

'He, he!' he said. 'That will teach you to say that the goblin is more clever than me!'

'Oh, but perhaps the goblin can make himself *smaller* than you can!' said Hop.

The wizard snorted crossly.

'That he can't!' he said. 'Why, I can make myself small enough to sit in that pudding-basin!'

'Surely not!' said Hop, Skip and Jump together.

'I'll just show you!' said the wizard. He rubbed some ointment on his forehead out of a yellow box. At once he began to shrink!

Smaller and smaller he grew until he was the size of a doll.

'Put me on the table!' he squeaked to the brownies. Skip put him there. He jumped into the pudding-basin and sat down.

'Wonderful! Wonderful!' cried Hop. 'You can't grow any smaller, of course.

'That I can!' squeaked the wizard.

'Small enough to sit in a tea-cup?' asked Hop.

The wizard rubbed some more ointment on his forehead. He grew smaller still, and jumped into a tea-cup.

'Simply marvellous!' said Hope, Skip, and Jump.

'I can grow smaller still,' squeaked the wizard.

'What, small enough to creep into this tiny bottle?' asked Hop, pretending to be greatly surprised, and holding out a very small bottle.

The wizard laughed, and at once became very tiny indeed – so tiny that he was able to creep through the neck of the little bottle and sit in it easily.

Then, quick as a flash, Hop picked up the cork and corked up the bottle!

'Ha!' he cried, in the greatest excitement. 'Now I've got you! Now you can't get out! Now you can't get out!'

The wizard shouted and yelled in his bottle, and struggled and kicked against the cork, but it wasn't a bit of good, not a bit.

'You're a wicked wizard,' said Skip, 'and now you've got your punishment!'

'Where's the wizard's stick?' asked Jump, looking round. 'Oh, there it is, leaning by his chair. Perhaps the wizard is powerless now and his stick will be harmless to us!'

He picked it up. It did nothing at all, but behaved just like an ordinary stick.

'Now to get out of here!' said Jump.

He swung the green stick three times into the air, and then let it fall on the ground.

At once the blue door appeared in one of the walls.

'Hurray!' cried Skip, and flung it open. 'Now we're free again!'

But, dear me! What a surprise they got when they ran out of the cottage – for, instead of being among the trees in the wood, it now stood on a sandy beach, and in front of the three brownies stretched a calm blue sea!

'Good gracious!' cried the brownies. 'What an extraordinary thing! The cottage must have been travelling for days!'

They looked out over the blue sea. Not a sail was to be seen.

'Well, I don't want to go exploring along this part of the country any more,' said Jump, 'in case we meet any more unpleasant wizards. I wish we could sail away on the sea!'

'I know,' cried Hop, 'let's get the table out of the cottage, and turn it upside down!'

'And use the table-cloth for a sail!' shouted Skip. 'And the magic stick for a mast!'

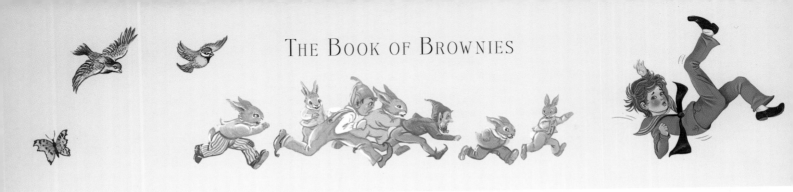

So into the cottage they went again, and dragged out the big table. They turned it upside down on the water and it floated beautifully. Then they set up the mast and fastened the table-cloth for a sail.

'Bring some of that purple and yellow ointment!' called Hop to Skip. 'It might come in useful!'

So the two boxes of ointment were fetched, and Hop put them into his pocket. Then, picking up the bottle with the angry little wizard inside, he pushed off their table-boat, jumped on it, and there were the brownies safe and sound on the calm, blue sea.

A tiny little breeze took them along, and they watched the wizard's cottage grow smaller and smaller in the distance.

'We'll keep the wizard with us,' said Hop. 'He might come in useful somehow, and so long as he's corked in the bottle, he's quite harmless.'

So he slipped the little bottle into his pocket along with the boxes of ointment.

On and on they went, rocking softly over the sea, till one by one they grew drowsy, and soon in the afternoon sun they fell asleep, whilst their strange little boat went sailing dreamily on.

Their Adventure
with the
Saucepan Man

The three brownies ran up to the jingling-jangling little man.

'Hello!' cried Hop. 'Are you the Saucepan Man?'

The little man looked at him inquiringly.

'Hey?' he said. 'What did you say?'

'Are you the Saucepan Man?' bawled Hop, over the jingling of scores of saucepans.

'No I ain't got a sausage-pan!' answered the Saucepan Man, shaking his head so that the saucepans rattled tremendously.

'Sausage-pan! I never said a *word* about a sausage-pan,' said Hop in surprise. 'I said, "Are you the Saucepan Man?"'

'I tell you I ain't got a sausage-pan,' said the little man crossly, 'I only sell saucepans, I do.'

'He's deaf,' said Skip, 'and I don't wonder, with all those saucepans jangling round him all day.'

Hop tried again. 'Are you the Saucepan Man?' he bawled. 'Can you hear me when I shout?'

'Yes, I think there's rain about,' said the Saucepan Man, looking up at the sky wisely.

'Come before evening too, likely enough.'

'*You* try, Skip,' said Hop, quite out of breath.

'WHERE ARE YOU GOING?' shouted Skip.

'Now don't be silly,' answered the Saucepan Man sharply. ''Tain't snowing, and you can see it ain't. Don't tell me any fairy-tales like that.'

'CAN WE GO HOME WITH YOU?' asked Jump in his most enormous voice.

'No, my boots ain't new, but what's that to do with you, I'd like to know?' said the little man, looking crosser and crosser.

'Oh, buttons and buttercups!' sighed Hop. 'We'll never make him hear, while he's got all those saucepans jangling round him. Let's follow him and see if he's going home. Then if he takes off his saucepans, we'll try again then.'

So the three brownies trotted behind the Saucepan Man, back down the lane again, and round by the station. There they saw the station-master and the porter, staring in great astonishment at the empty engine standing all by itself in the station.

'Gracious!' said Hop. 'Let's hope we don't get asked any awkward questions!'

The station-master saw them coming and immediately rushed over to them.

'Pretend we don't understand,' said Hop quickly

to the others. 'If we talk a lot of rubbish, he'll soon let us go.'

'Hi! Hi!' called the station-master. 'Do you know anything about this engine?'

Nobody answered anything.

'Are you dumb?' asked the station-master angrily. 'Come now! Do you know anything about this engine, I say?'

'Kalamma Koo, chickeree chee,' answered Hop solemnly.

'Krik-krik,' said Skip.

'Caw,' said Jump.

'*They* don't know anything, that's certain,' said the station-master to the porter. 'They're foreigners.'

'Tanee jug jug jug?' said Hop, in an inquiring voice.

'It's all right,' said the station-master. 'I don't understand you. I'll have a word with this sauce-pan chap.'

'Caw, caw,' said Jump, and nearly made the others giggle.

The station-master poked the Saucepan Man in the ribs.

'Hi!' he cried. 'Do you know anything about this engine?'

'My name ain't Benjamin, and kindly take your

fingers out of my waistcoat,' said the Saucepan Man huffily.

The station-master groaned.

'Come on,' he said to the porter. 'They're quite mad – too mad to know anything about an engine, *any*way!'

They went off to the station again, and the three brownies breathed freely once more.

'That was a near squeak!' said Hop. 'Come on, and let's follow the Saucepan Man.'

On they went again, until at last the Saucepan Man came to a little tumbledown cottage, called Saucepan Cottage. It had old saucepans for its chimneys, and looked the funniest little place the brownies had ever seen. They followed the Saucepan Man inside. He looked at them in surprise.

'What do you want?' he asked.

Hop suddenly saw that the table was very dusty. He quickly wrote on it with his finger.

'We are three brownies who want to know the way to Witchland,' he wrote. 'The Very Wise Man told us to ask the Saucepan Man the way. Are you the Saucepan Man?'

'Course I am,' said the little man. 'Can't you *see* that? Anyway, I don't know why you didn't ask me that in the road, instead of talking about sausage-pans and the weather.'

He took off his saucepans and clattered them into a corner.

'I can tell you the way to Witchland all right,' he said. 'In fact, I'm on my way there tomorrow. You'd better come with me, you'll be safe then. Witches don't touch me, they don't.'

'Why not?' asked Hop.

'Feel hot, do you?' said the little man. 'Well, open the window then.'

Hop sighed. It really was *very* difficult to talk to the Saucepan Man. He tried again.

'May we spend the night here?' he asked in his loudest voice.

'What's the matter with my right ear?' said the Saucepan Man, going to the looking-glass, and peering into it. 'Nothing at all. Don't you be saucy, young man.'

'I can't stand this!' groaned Hop to the others. 'Haven't you got a note-book that we can write in?'

'Yes, *I* have!' cried Skip, pulling out an old note-book and a stumpy pencil. 'Here you are — write in this, Hop.'

Hop quickly wrote down his questions, and showed them to the Saucepan Man.

'Yes, you can stay here for the night,' said the little man, 'and I'll take you with me tomorrow. Find the cocoa tin now and make some cocoa,

while I boil some eggs and make some toast.'

The brownies hunted about for the cocoa, filled one of the many saucepans with milk and put it on the fire to boil.

Soon the four were enjoying boiled eggs, toast and cocoa, and the brownies began to think the Saucepan Man was a very jolly little man, for although he couldn't hear very well, he could tell lots of funny tales.

'Now to bed, to bed!' he said at last. 'We've a long way to go tomorrow and we must be up early.'

He showed them a bedroom with a big bed in it, said goodnight, and shut the door.

'Well, I really feel we're on the way to find the Princess Peronel now,' said Hop, as he got into bed.

'Yes, if the Saucepan Man takes us to Witchland, we've only got to find out where Witch Green-eyes lives, and then make up a plan to rescue the Princess,' said Skip sleepily.

'Well, goodnight,' said Jump, yawning. All the brownies lay down and fell fast asleep.

In the morning the Saucepan Man woke them, and they started off on their journey. They walked for miles across the country, calling at little cottages on the way, and selling saucepans.

Soon Hop had a good idea. He took out his little note-book and wrote in it.

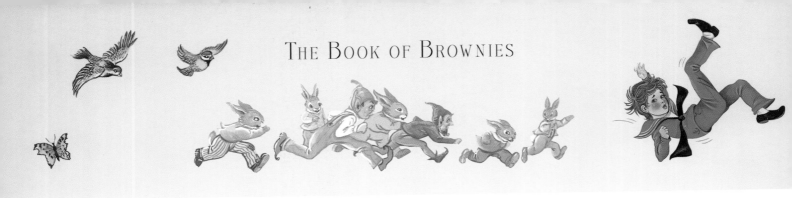

'Let us carry your saucepans for you for a little while,' Hop wrote. 'You must be very tired, for the sun is hot.'

The Saucepan Man gladly took off all his saucepans and gave them to the three brownies. They divided the saucepans between them, and off they all went again, clinking and clanking for all the world as if they were saucepan men themselves.

Suddenly, as they were going along, a great shadow came over them, and made everything dark.

The brownies looked up and saw an enormous yellow bird hovering over them. The Saucepan Man gave a frightened yell.

'Run!' he said 'Run! It's the Dragon-bird that belongs to the Golden Dwarf. Don't let him get you!'

The brownies sped away to some trees. The Saucepan Man didn't seem to know *where* to go. He ran forwards and backwards, and sideways, and all the time the Dragon-bird hovered overhead like a great hawk.

Then zee-ee-ee! It swooped downwards so fast that its feathers made a singing noise. The brownies saw it get hold of the poor little Saucepan Man, and then the Dragon-bird rose into the air, taking him in its talons.

THEIR ADVENTURE WITH THE SAUCEPAN MAN

'Oh my! Oh my!' cried Hop in despair. 'It's got him! It's got him!'

'Poor little Saucepan Man,' sobbed Skip, tears pouring down his face.

'Look! Look! It's flying towards that hill over there,' said Jump.

The brownies watched. On the top of the faraway hill was a castle. The Dragon-bird flew to the highest window there, landed, and disappeared into the castle.

'*Now* what are we to do?' said Hop mournfully.

'We can't go on and leave him,' said Skip, drying his eyes. 'Besides, we've got his saucepans.'

'Oh, isn't it bad luck that this should happen, just as we were really on our way to Witchland!' sighed Jump. 'Look at that signpost there. It says "THIS WAY TO WITCHLAND" on it.'

'Well, we'd better go to that hill over there,' said Skip bravely. 'We might be able to rescue the Saucepan Man *some*how. We simply *can't* leave him to that Dragon-bird and the Golden Dwarf.'

'Come on then,' said Hop, and off they all went, keeping a very sharp look-out in case the Dragon-bird came back again.

The hill was very much farther away than it looked. All the afternoon the brownies travelled, their saucepans clanking and jingling at every step.

'No wonder the Saucepan Man is so deaf!' said Hop. 'It's all I can do to hear myself speak with all this noise going on.'

Presently they came to a little cottage.

'Let's knock at the door,' said Skip, 'and see if we can get some food in exchange for a saucepan. I'm hungry.'

They knocked. A dwarf opened the door and peered at them.

'What do you want?' he said.

'Do you want any saucepans?' asked Hop. 'We've got some fine ones here.'

'How much?' asked the dwarf.

'We'll give you a big one, if you'll give us a loaf, and some milk,' said Hop.

The dwarf fetched them three cups of milk and a loaf of bread.

'Here you are,' he said. 'Now give me your biggest saucepan.'

Hop gave him a fine blue saucepan.

'Who lives in that castle over there on that hill?' he asked.

'The Golden Dwarf,' answered their customer. 'Don't you go there, or you'll be captured by the Dragon-bird.'

'Why does the Golden Dwarf capture people?' asked Skip.

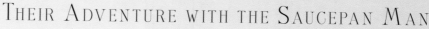

'To eat,' answered the dwarf. 'Didn't you know *that*? Ah, he's a terrible fellow, the Golden Dwarf is, I can tell you. There's only one word that will stop him in his evil ways, but as he lives away up there in his high castle that nobody can enter, he's safe!'

'What's the word?' asked Hop with interest.

'Ho ho! Don't you wish you could use it on the Golden Dwarf!' laughed the dwarf. 'Well, I'll tell you. It's "Kerolamisticootalimarcawnokeeto"!'

'Buttons and buttercups!' said Hop. 'I'll never be able to say that!'

'We'll split it into three and each of us can remember a bit of it!' said Skip cleverly.

The dwarf laughed, and said the long word again. Hop said the first piece over and over to himself, while Skip said the middle bit and Jump repeated the last bit.

'Much good it'll do you!' said the dwarf. 'Why, no one's ever even *seen* the Golden Dwarf since I've lived here – and I've been here a hundred and forty-three years come next November!'

The brownies sighed. Things seemed very difficult. They said goodbye and left the cottage behind them.

'*Is* it any good going to the castle?' said Jump, who was beginning to feel very down in the

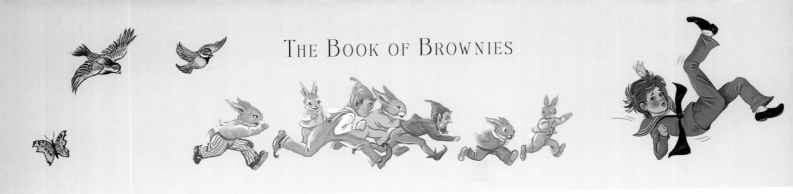

dumps. 'Suppose we all get caught and eaten.'

'Cheer up,' said Hop. 'You can only get eaten *once*, you know!'

'Don't be silly,' said Jump crossly. 'I don't want to be eaten even once.'

'Sh!' said Skip. 'We're getting near the castle. Better keep a good look-out.'

'Bother the clanking saucepans,' said Hop. 'Shall we take them off and leave them here?'

'No,' said Skip. 'If that horrid Dragon-bird appears again we'll pretend we're just a heap of old tins, and maybe it won't see us then.'

Just as he spoke a shadow fell over them again. At once the three sank down to the ground beneath their saucepans, and lay quite still. The shadow grew blacker, and at last the Dragon-bird landed by them with a flop. It pecked at Skip's saucepans and dented them badly. Then it spread its wings, rose into the air, and flew away again.

'Oh my stars!' said Jump, shaking like a jelly. 'This is the sort of adventure that doesn't agree with me at all. Has that horrid bird gone?'

'Yes,' said Hop. 'It's a nasty-looking thing too, I can tell you. It's got scales as well as feathers, and a long tail. It must have thought we were piles of saucepans!'

'Come on while we're safe,' said Skip.

They ran towards the castle and, panting and breathless, flung themselves down at the foot of it.

'Isn't it a funny colour!' said Hop, looking at it closely. 'It looks just like toffee!'

Skip broke a piece off and licked it.

'It *is* toffee!' he said. 'My goodness! Fancy a castle built of toffee!'

'Toffee!' cried Jump in delight. 'I say, how lovely! I'm going to have a really big bit!'

He broke off a fine fat piece and began chewing it. It was delicious.

'I suppose it was built by magic,' said Hop. 'I can't imagine *people* building it, can you? They'd get so terribly sticky.'

'Well, don't let's forget about the Saucepan Man,' said Skip, looking round about him. 'I expect he's feeling very lonely and afraid.'

'Let's explore round the outside of the castle,' said Hop. 'Maybe we can find some way of getting in then.'

Off went the brownies, after having carefully taken off the saucepans and hidden them under a bush. They were afraid that the Golden Dwarf might hear the clanking if they carried them about.

They marched off round the toffee castle, looking everywhere for a window or a door.

Not one was to be seen.

'Goodness!' said Hop at last. 'No wonder nobody ever sees the Golden Dwarf, if there's no window and no door on the ground-floor.'

'I don't believe there's any way of getting into the castle at all except by that window right at the very top,' said Skip, craning his neck to see.

He was right. Not a door was to be seen, and no windows either, except the big one set right at the very top of the castle, where the Dragon-bird had flown in with the Saucepan Man.

The brownies came back to their saucepans and sat down under the bush.

'Well, that *is* a puzzle,' said Hop. 'We haven't a ladder, and there's no door – so how ever *can* we get in?'

'We can't,' said Jump. 'The only thing left to do is to go back to that signpost, and take the road to Witchland.'

'What, and leave the poor old Saucepan Man to be eaten by the Golden Dwarf?' cried Skip, who was very tender-hearted. 'After he's been so very kind to us too!'

The others looked uncomfortable. They didn't like leaving their friend behind, but they didn't really see what else there was to do.

'Listen!' said Skip. 'If you want something badly enough, you're sure to find out a way. Now

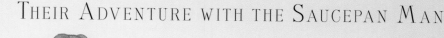

let's just keep quiet and think very, very hard.'

The three brownies put their heads on their hands, shut they eyes, and thought.

They thought and thought and thought.

The sun went down. Still the brownies thought.

The moon came up. Still the brownies thought.

Then Hop raised his head. 'If only we could get something to climb up the wall with,' he said. 'But we haven't anything at all.'

'Except silly old saucepans,' said Jump mournfully.

'Yes – saucepans,' repeated Hop. Then his eyes widened as a great thought came into his head.

'*Saucepans*!' he said again, and chuckled. Then he got up and did a little dance of joy. Skip and Jump stared at him in astonishment.

'Are you mad, Hop?' asked Skip.

'Or do you feel ill?' asked Jump.

'No, I'm not mad!' answered Hop. 'I've only got that fantastic feeling you get when you suddenly think of a perfectly splendid idea.'

'What is it?' asked Skip and Jump together.

'Well, here we've been groaning and moaning because we've nothing to get us up the castle wall,' said Hop, 'and we've got the very best thing in the world to get us up there – the saucepans!'

'Whatever *do* you mean?' asked Skip.

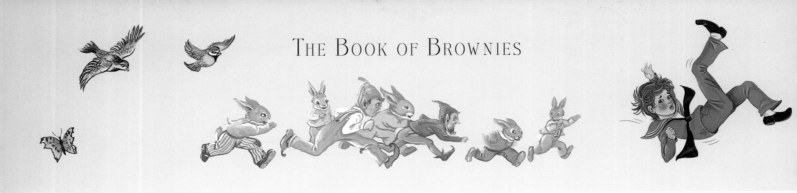
'*This* is what I mean,' said Hop, and he picked up a saucepan. He held it upside down and drove the handle into the toffee wall. It went in quite easily, and stayed there, for the toffee held it tight.

'One step up,' said Hop, and picked up another saucepan. He pushed the handle of that one in, a little way above the first one.

'Two steps up!' he cried. '*Now* do you see the idea?'

'Oh *yes*!' cried the other two. 'What a good plan, Hop! We can climb up on the saucepans, if only the handles will hold all right!'

'The toffee will hold them,' laughed Hop, who was beginning to feel very excited.

One by one the saucepans' handles were driven into the wall, so that every saucepan made a step higher than the last. They were quite firm and steady and, as the brownies were little and light, there was no fear of the steps breaking.

Higher and higher they went, until they had almost reached the window at the top. Jump carried the saucepans that were left and passed them one by one to Skip, who passed them to Hop, who drove the handles into the wall.

'What a mercy we had so many saucepans!' whispered Skip.

'Yes, wasn't it!' said Hop. 'I say! We're nearly

at the top. Suppose the Golden Dwarf leans out of the window and sees us!'

'We'll say the magic word!' said Skip. 'I know my bit all right.'

'And I know mine!' said Jump.

'Well, we'll have to join the bits on very quickly when we say it,' said Hop, 'or else it won't sound like a word. Perhaps we'd better practise it before we go any further.'

'Hurry up, then,' said Skip, 'I'm not very anxious to hang on to these saucepans all night.'

Hop said his part of the magic word, Skip said the middle and Jump joined in quickly with the end. After seven or eight times they managed to do it perfectly, and Hop thought they might go on.

They had just enough saucepans to reach to the window-ledge. At last Hop could peep over it and look into the room.

He saw a large room hung with golden curtains and spread with a golden carpet. In the middle of it, sitting on a stool, was the Saucepan Man, looking the picture of misery. He was all alone.

'Good!' said Hop, and whispered what he saw to the others. Then he peeped over the ledge again.

The Saucepan Man looked up and when he saw Hop, he fell off his stool in astonishment.

'I must be dreaming,' he said, and pinched himself very hard.

'Ow!' he said. 'No, I'm not.'

He ran to the window.

'Help me over,' said Hop. 'We've come to rescue you.'

The Saucepan Man hauled him into the room, and then they helped Skip and Jump.

Quickly, Hop wrote in his notebook to tell the Saucepan Man how they had come to him.

'You'd better escape at once, with us,' wrote Hop, 'for there's no knowing when that awful Dragon-bird will appear again, or the Golden Dwarf.'

'Ugh! Don't talk of them,' begged the Saucepan Man. 'I shall never forget being carried off in those talons. When I got here the Golden Dwarf came and looked at me, and said I wouldn't be plump enough to eat for a week.'

The brownies shivered.

'Come on,' said Hop, running to the window. 'Let's escape while we can.'

He had just got one leg over the window-sill, when heavy footsteps outside the door made his hair stand on end.

'Oh!' whispered the Saucepan Man. 'Hide, quick! It's the Golden Dwarf.'

The brownies dived behind one of the curtains just as the door opened. In came a peculiar creature, not much bigger than the brownies, who looked as if he were made of solid gold. Hop thought he looked more like a statue than a live person.

'I smell brownies!' said the Golden Dwarf suddenly, and sniffed the air.

The three brownies trembled.

'Remember the magic word,' whispered Hop anxiously. 'It's our only chance.'

'I SMELL BROWNIES!' said the Golden Dwarf again, and strode over to the shaking curtain.

He pulled it aside. Out sprang Hop, Skip, and Jump. 'Kerolamisti –' shouted Hop.

'Cootalimar –' went on Skip.

'Cawnokeeto!' finished Jump.

The Golden Dwarf stared at them in terror.

'The Word! The Word!' he cried, and pulled at his hair. Then he uttered a deep groan, jumped into the air, and vanished completely.

The brownies and the Saucepan Man stared at the place where the Golden Dwarf had stood. Nothing happened. He didn't come back.

'You've done the trick!' said the Saucepan Man. 'He's gone for good!'

'Hurrah!' cried Hop. 'Thank goodness we remembered the magic word! Come on, Saucepan

Man – let's get away from this horrid castle!'

Over the window-sill they clambered, and were soon scrambling down the saucepans as fast as they could go. 'We'll leave them there,' said the Saucepan Man. 'I don't want to waste any more time here, in case the Dragon-bird comes back.'

So off they all went in the moonlight, to the signpost pointing to Witchland.

Their Adventure on the Green Railway

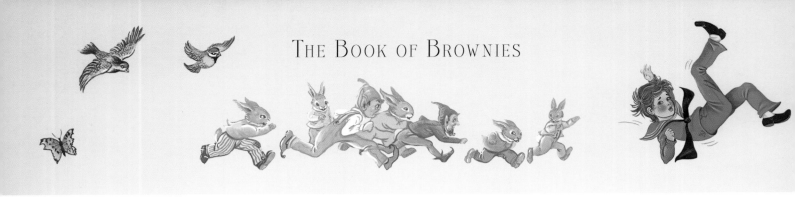

The brownies looked around. They were in a bare, open country, with the walls of the Land of the Clever People behind them.

'We'd better see you safely back to your country first,' said Hop to the little girl, who was dancing about and clapping her hands for joy at having escaped.

'Oh, we'll all travel on the Green Railway,' said the little girl. 'I'll get out at Giggleswick – that's my station – and you can go on to Fiddlestick Field if you like, or come and stay with me at my home.'

'I think we'd better not do that,' said Hop, who was beginning to feel that it was far easier to get *into* a strange land than *out* of it. 'We might not giggle enough.'

'Besides, we want to find out the way to Witchland as soon as we can,' said Skip, 'so that we can rescue poor little Princess Peronel.'

'Well, first of all, where's the Green Railway?' asked Jump.

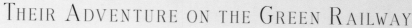 

'Oh, it runs beneath the ground just here,' explained the little girl. 'I'll show you how to get to it. Look for a big yellow mushroom, all of you.'

The brownies began hunting all around.

'I've found a beauty!' cried Hop.

'So have I!' called Skip.

'So have we,' said the little girl, running up with Jump. 'Bring them here and set them down in a circle.'

They all brought their mushrooms. They were very big ones, quite as large as stools, and the brownies were able to stand them up straight, and then sit on the tops.

'Hold tight to your mushrooms,' said the little girl, 'while I say a magic rhyme.'

The brownies held tight.

'Mushrooms, take us down below;
One, two, three, and off we go.
Rikky, tikky, tolly vo!'

cried the little girl.

Whizz-whizz-whizz! The mushrooms suddenly sank down through the ground at a terrific pace. The brownies gasped for breath and held on as tightly as ever they could.

Then bump-bump-bump-bump — the four

mushrooms all came to a sudden stop and tipped the brownies off their seats. They rolled on the ground.

'Ha, ha!' laughed the little girl, who was still sitting on her mushroom. 'Anyone can see you're not used to riding mushrooms. Come along, and we'll see if a train is due now.'

The brownies picked themselves up and followed the little girl, who was scampering through a cave lit by one star-shaped lamp.

When she came to the end of it she stopped, and the brownies saw a little door let into the wall. It opened, and the little girl ran through it. The brownies followed her and, to their astonishment, found themselves on a tiny little platform.

A solemn grey rabbit sat there with piles of tickets in front of him.

'One to Giggleswick and three to Fiddlestick Field,' said the little girl.

'One silver coin each,' said the grey rabbit, handing out the four tickets. 'Next train in five minutes.'

Sure enough, in five minutes there came the rattle and clank of a train, and the funniest little engine ran into the station, dragging behind it a long row of higgledy-piggledy carriages. They had no roof and no seats – only just cushions on the floor.

It was a very crowded train. One carriage was full of velvety moles, who talked about the best way to catch beetles. Another carriage was full of giggling people, who seemed to be making jokes and laughing at them as fast as they could.

'Oh, there are some of my own people!' cried the little girl gladly. 'They're going to Giggleswick, I expect. Let's get in with them.'

So they all jumped in with the laughing people, though the brownies would really rather have got into an empty carriage.

The train went off when the guard waved his flag and blew his whistle. It ran clanking through dark tunnels, and big and little caves. The brownies were very much interested in all they saw and would have liked to talk about it – but the other people in the carriage were so talkative, and laughed so often, that they couldn't get a word in.

The little girl was very excited; she laughed more than anyone, and told all about her adventures in the Land of Clever People. Hop thought she was nicer *in* that land than out of it, because she didn't giggle so much then.

The train stopped again.

'Burrow Corner!' shouted a sandy rabbit-porter.

The moles all got out, and so did the grey bunnies. Then the train went off again.

The next station was Giggleswick. All the Gigglers got out. The little girl flung her arms round each of the brownies and hugged them.

'Do, do, *do* come and stay in my country,' she begged. 'Jump out now, do! We're very merry and laugh all day!'

'No, we really mustn't,' said Hop, who didn't want to go with the Gigglers in the least. 'Goodbye, and we're *so* glad you're safe home again.'

The train rattled off, and the brownies waved goodbye.

'Well!' said Jump, sitting down on his cushion. 'I think I'd rather have to speak in rhyme all day than giggle every minute. What a terrible country to live in!'

'Thank goodness we didn't go there!' said Hop. 'What a lot of peculiar lands there are outside Fairyland! How I wish we could go back to dear old Brownie Town again!'

'So do I,' said Skip, with a sigh. 'But I don't expect we'll ever be able to do that, because we shall never be able to find our goodnesses, as the King said we must.'

'Oh look!' said Jump. 'We're coming out into the open air again!'

The train puffed out of the half-darkness and came to a sunny field. It ran along beside a hedge

for some way, and then out on a roadway. All sorts of strange folk were walking there, and all kinds of animals, who looked as if they had been out marketing.

The train stopped whenever anybody hailed it, and lots of people got in.

'We shall never get to Fiddlestick Field,' said Hop, when the train stopped for the fifteenth time. 'Really, people are treating this train more like a bus! Oh dear, what's happened now?'

The train stopped again. The driver was having a long talk with a friend he had met. The brownies got very impatient.

At last Hop got out and went up to the driver.

'Aren't we ever going on again?' he asked. 'We're in a hurry.'

'Oh, are you?' said the driver. 'Well, I'm going to have tea with my friend here, so you'd better get out and walk. This train won't start till six o'clock.'

So saying, the driver jumped from the train, linked his arm in his friend's and strolled off.

All the passengers yawned, settled themselves on their cushions, and went to sleep. The three brownies were very cross.

'Fine sort of train this is!' grumbled Skip. 'Goodness knows when we'll get to Fiddlestick Field!'

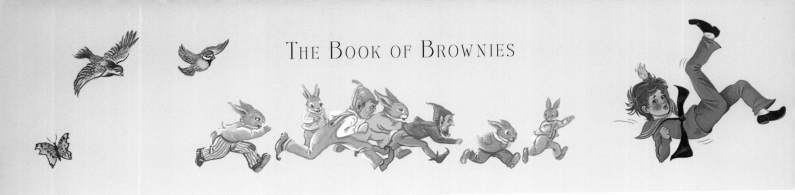

'I've a jolly good mind to drive the train myself,' said Hop.

'Oh, Hop, *do*!' cried Jump. 'I'm sure you could. Then we could get to Fiddlestick Field tonight.'

Hop looked at the engine. It really didn't look very difficult to drive, and he had always longed to be an engine-driver. This seemed a lovely chance.

'All right,' he said. 'Come on! I'll drive the train, with you to help me. How pleased all the passengers will be!'

Hop, Skip and Jump ran to the engine, and jumped into the cabin. There were four wheels there, like the steering wheels of motor-cars, and Hop had a good look at them.

Over one was written 'Turn to the left' and over another, 'Turn to the right'. The third wheel had 'Go fast' written over it and the last wheel had 'Start engine'.

'Oh well, this all looks easy enough,' said Hop, twisting the 'Start engine' wheel. 'Now we'll go on our travels once more!'

The train started off, rattle-clank, rattle!

All the passengers woke up and looked most surprised. They hadn't expected the train to go so soon. One of them looked to see why the driver had come back so quickly.

'Good gracious!' he cried. 'Those brownies are

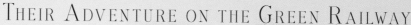

driving! We shall have an accident!'

Everyone looked over the edge of their carriages in alarm. Yes, sure enough, the brownies were driving the engine. Dear, dear, dear!

'We're coming to a curve!' said Skip, who was thoroughly enjoying himself. 'Twist the "Turn to the left" wheel, Jump!'

Jump did so, and the train went smoothly round the bend. The brownies felt very pleased with themselves indeed. Fancy being able to drive an engine without any practice!

'We *must* be clever!' they thought.

'There's a station coming!' shouted Jump. 'Slow down, Hop, and stop, in case anyone wants to get out here.'

But dear me! There wasn't any wheel that said 'Slow down' or 'Stop'! Even when they twisted the 'Start engine' wheel backwards, the train didn't slow down.

Whiz-z-z! The station rushed by and the train didn't stop.

Some of the passengers were very angry, for they wanted to get out, and they began shouting and yelling at Hop for all they were worth. They made him so nervous that instead of twisting the 'Turn to the right! wheel, when he came to another bend in the line, he twisted the "Go fast" wheel.

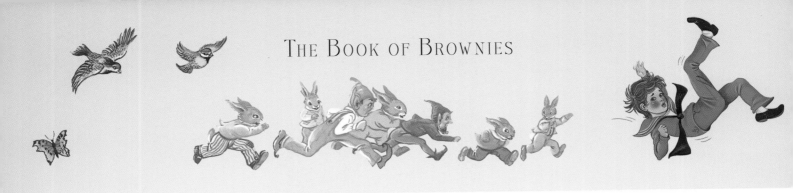

Br-rr-rr-rr! The engine leaped forward and raced along the rails as if it were mad. All the carriages rocked and rattled, and the passengers' hats flew off in the air.

'Hop! Hop!' shouted Skip, in a fright. 'We shall have an accident. Make it go slow!'

But there wasn't any wheel that said 'Go slow' and Hop didn't know what in the world to do. He twisted every wheel in turn, but nothing happened at all, except that the train seemed to go faster. The wind whistled past the brownies' ears and took their breath away.

Stations whizzed past. The passengers forgot their anger in fear and clutched at the sides of their rocking carriages. A rabbit had his whiskers blown right off, and was terribly upset.

Then the train went up a big hill. It went more slowly, and some of the passengers wondered whether they would risk jumping out. There was a station at the top of the hill, and Hop read the name.

'Fiddlestick Field!' he cried. 'Oh dear, this is where we get out. Oh, can't we stop the train somehow?'

But he couldn't and the station went past. The train reached the hill-top, and began going down the other side.

The three brownies sat down suddenly, as the engine started tearing downhill.

'It's like a switchback!' groaned Hop. 'Oh dear! It's climbing up another hill now!'

'And here's another station,' said Skip, leaning out. 'Oh my! Switchback Station! I hope to goodness we're not going to go up and down like this much longer. It makes me feel quite ill.'

The train tore downhill again, then up and then down once more. The carriages followed in a rattling row, while all the passengers shrieked and shouted. Stations raced by, but the train didn't

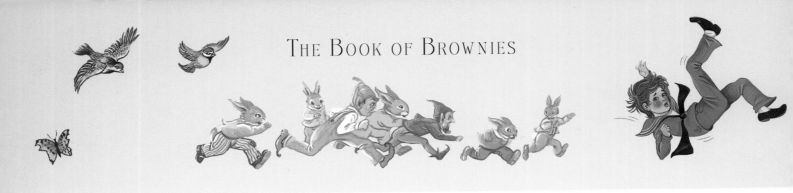

seem to think of stopping anywhere.

'Horrid little engine!' said Hop. 'I believe it's thoroughly enjoying itself!'

'Oh my!' shouted Skip suddenly. 'The engine's gone off the rails! Oh my!'

'And there's a pond in front of us!' yelled Jump. 'Oh!'

Ker-splash! Ker-plunk! Into the pond went the engine, carriages and passengers. Everybody was tumbled, splash! into the pond, and the noise frightened all the ducks away to the bank.

'Splutter-splutter!' went everyone, floundering about in the shallow, muddy water. No one was hurt, but everybody was very, very angry.

'Catch those brownies!' they yelled, and made a grab at Hop, Skip and Jump. 'Take them to prison!'

The brownies scrambled out of the pond as quickly as they could. They began to feel frightened when they heard the angry voices of all the passengers. There were rabbits, moles, weasels, Gigglers, two Clever People, a peddler with a sack, and some peculiar people who didn't look as if they belonged to anywhere.

They all scrambled out of the pond after the brownies and chased them. Down the lane went the three, followed by all the passengers.

'Stop them! Stop them!' they cried.

The brownies raced on. Soon they came to a strange little village, built entirely of large mushrooms and toadstools. They had doors in the stalks, and windows and chimneys in the top part.

Little people came to the doors and looked out when they heard all the noise. They stared in astonishment at the sight of the three running brownies, followed by all the other people.

At the end of the village ran a stream. It was too wide and too deep for the brownies to cross, and they didn't know *what* to do.

'Quick, quick! Think of something!' cried Skip.

Hop looked round despairingly. The passengers were almost on them. Then a clever thought came to him.

He ran to a toadstool, snapped it off, put it upside down on the stream, and jumped into it. Skip and Jump sprang in just in time, pushed off from the bank, and left the passengers staring at them in dismay.

'Ha, ha!' called Hop, feeling very relieved. 'You didn't get us *that* time!'

'No, but someone else will get you! Look behind you!' yelled the rabbit whose whiskers had been blown off.

The brownies looked on to the other bank, and who do you think stood there? Why, three wooden-

looking soldiers, all waiting for the toadstool boat to land!

Bump! The toadstool reached the shore. The soldiers sprang forward, caught hold of each of the brownies and marched them off.

'Now, quick march!' said the soldiers sternly. 'You'll go to prison till tomorrow morning, and then be brought before the judge for frightening our ducks, and for using one of our houses for a boat.'

The brownies wriggled and struggled, but it was no good. They were marched into a toad-stool marked PRISON, and there they were locked in for the night.

'Oh dear, dear, dear!' wept Jump. 'I'm wet and cold and hungry. Hop, you've got us into trouble *again*!'

'Be quiet!' said Hop, who was feeling very much ashamed of himself and of his doings in the train.

'Goodnight,' said Skip sadly. 'I'm going to sleep to see if I can't find something to eat in my dreams.'

And in two minutes the bad brownies were fast asleep.

Their Adventure
with the Labeller
and the Bottler

They hadn't gone very far when the Saucepan Man began to yawn.

'I'm *so* sleepy,' he said, 'and it really must be very late. What about getting underneath a bush and going to sleep till morning?'

The brownies thought it would be a very good idea. So they all cuddled together beneath a bush, and went fast asleep till the sun rose.

'Wake up! Wake up!' cried Hop. 'It's time to go on our way to Witchland and rescue the Princess Peronel.'

The others woke with a jump. They washed in a nearby stream, picked some blackberries for breakfast and went on towards the sign-post.

Suddenly a great black shadow came over them.

'Oh! Oh!' yelled the Saucepan Man in terror. 'It's the Dragon-bird again. Run! Run!'

The brownies ran helter-skelter to some bushes. The black shadow grew darker.

Zee-ee-ee! The Dragon-bird landed on the ground by them with a thud.

'Where is my master? Where is my master?' it cried in a croaking voice.

'We have said a magic word and made him vanish for ever!' shouted Hop bravely. 'And if you don't leave us alone, we'll make *you* vanish too, you horrid Dragon-bird.'

'No, no!' shrieked the bird. 'Oh, most powerful wizard, let me serve *you*, now that my master the Golden Dwarf, is gone. Let me be your slave.'

'Gracious!' said Hop. 'Here is a to-do! Goodness knows we don't a Dragon-bird always at our heels, begging to be our slave.'

The Saucepan Man, who seemed to hear the Dragon-bird quite well, crawled out from under his bush and walked up to it.

'Go away!' he said. 'If we want you we will call you. Don't come bothering us now, or we will make you disappear, as we did your master.'

'I will come if ever you want me,' croaked the bird sadly. 'I will await that time.'

It spread its wings, rose into the air, and in a few moments was out of sight.

'That was rather a nasty shock,' said Hop.

'I quite thought it would take us all away again. Ugh! I hope we never see the ugly thing any more!'

'So do *we*!' said Skip and Jump.

'Come on,' said the Saucepan Man, and once

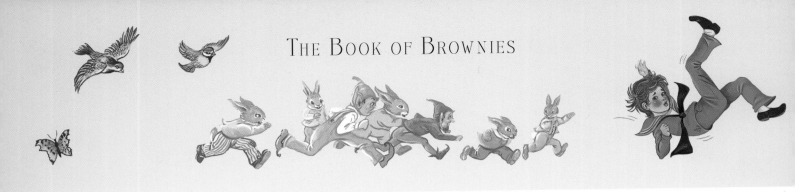

more the four set off to the signpost.

At last they reached it, and set off down the road towards Witchland.

'Don't you bother to come with us,' said Hop to the Saucepan Man. 'We can find our way quite well now.'

'No, I can't hear any bell,' said the Saucepan Man, standing still to listen. 'You must be mistaken.'

'Oh dear, you *are* deaf!' sighed Hop, and quickly wrote down what he had said.

'Ho, ho!' laughed the Saucepan Man. 'So you think you could find the way by yourself, do you? Ho, ho! You just follow me, and you'll soon see you couldn't find the way alone!'

No sooner had he said that than the four travellers came to a river. Over it stretched a graceful bridge but, to the brownies' surprise, no sooner did they get near it than the end nearest to them raised itself and stayed there.

'How annoying of it!' said Hop, in surprise. 'What does it do that for? We can't get across!'

'Don't worry!' said the Saucepan Man. He looked about on the ground and picked up four tiny blue stones. He threw them into the river one after the other, saying a magic word at each of them.

At once the end of the bridge came down again, and rested on the bank.

'There you are,' said the Saucepan Man. 'Now we can cross.'

The brownies ran across quickly, just in case the bridge took it into its head to do anything funny again.

They hadn't gone very far beyond the bridge before they came to a forest so dark and so thick that the brownies felt sure they couldn't possibly get through it. They tried this way and that way, but it was all no good – they could not find a path.

The Saucepan Man watched them, laughing.

Then he quickly ran to a big white stone lying nearby and lifted it up. Underneath it lay a coil of silver string. The Saucepan Man took it up and tied one end to a tree-trunk.

Then he said a magic rhyme, and immediately, to the brownies' great surprise, the string uncoiled and went sliding away all by itself into the dark forest.

'Follow it quickly!' cried the Saucepan Man, and ran into the forest.

The silver string gleamed through the bushes and trees, and led the brownies by a hidden, narrow path through the dark forest. On and on they went, following the silver thread, until at

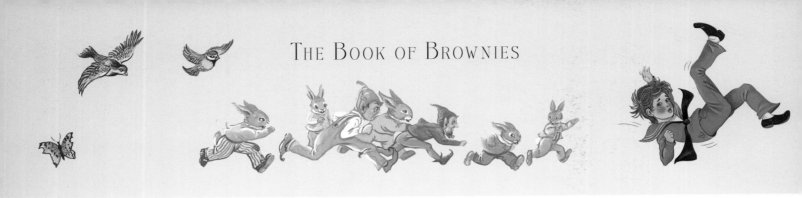

last they reached the end of the trees, and stood in sunshine once more.

'I don't know what we should do without you,' shouted Hop to the Saucepan Man. 'We should never have known the way!'

'*Who's* making hay?' asked the Saucepan Man, staring all round about him.

'No one!' shouted Hop, and wrote in his notebook to tell the Saucepan Man what he was talking about.

Presently they set off again. In the distance they saw an enormous hill. As they drew nearer the brownies saw it gleaming and glittering, as if it were made of ice.

'Glass,' explained the Saucepan Man, as they drew near.

'I wonder how we get up *that*!' said Hop.

The brownies tried to climb it, but as fast as they tried, down them came, ker-plunk, to the bottom!

'Tell us how to get up!' Hop wrote in his notebook, to the Saucepan Man.

Their guide smiled. He took six paces to the left, picked up a yellow stone, and aimed it carefully at a notch in the glass hill.

As soon as it struck the notch, a door slid open in the hillside and the brownies saw a passage leading through the glass hill.

'It's easier to go through than up,' smiled the Saucepan Man, leading the way.

The passage was very strange, for it wound about like a river. The sides, top and bottom were all glass, and reflected everything so perfectly that the brownies kept walking into the walls, and bumping their noses.

They were very glad when at last they came out at the other side of the hill. In front of them towered a great gate, and on it was written in iron lettering:

WITCHLAND

'At last!' said Hop. 'Now we really have arrived!'

'Here I must leave you,' said the Saucepan Man sadly. 'I cannot go in and I don't know how *you'll* get in either. But you are so clever, that maybe you'll find a way. Now I must go back and make some more saucepans to sell.'

'Thank you for bringing us here,' wrote Hop in his notebook. 'We are sorry to say goodbye.'

'So am I,' said the Saucepan Man, with tears in his eyes. 'Thank you very much for all your goodness to me in rescuing me from the Golden Dwarf.'

'Don't mention it,' said the brownies politely.

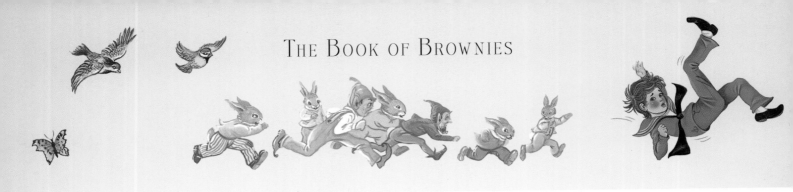

Then the Saucepan Man shook hands solemnly with them all, and said goodbye.

'Goodbye, goodbye!' called the brownies, as he went towards the glass hill.

He turned round.

'What sort of pie?' he called in surprise.

'Oh buttons and buttercups, isn't he deaf!' said Hop, and waved to the Saucepan Man to go on.

They watched him disappear into the hill.

'Nice old Saucepan Man,' said Skip. 'Wish he was coming to Witchland with us.'

'I wonder how we get in!' said Hop, looking at the tall gates.

'Don't know,' said Skip. 'We'd better wait until someone goes in or out, and then try and slip in as the gates open. Let's sit down under the may-tree and wait.'

They sat down and waited.

Nobody went either in or out of the gates. The brownies felt very bored.

Hop looked all round to see if anyone was in sight. He suddenly saw something in the distance.

'Look!' he said. 'There's a procession or something coming. We could easily slip in with that when the gates open for it, couldn't we?'

'Yes!' said Jump. 'Let's wait quietly and then try our luck.'

The procession came nearer. At the same time somebody came from the opposite direction. Skip looked to see who it was.

'It's a little brown mouse!' he said in surprise. 'I wonder what a mouse is doing here! He seems to be carrying a heavy sack, look!'

The others looked. The little mouse was certainly carrying a sack that seemed far too heavy for him.

The procession and the mouse reached the place where the brownies sat, just at the same moment. The procession was made up of all sorts of strange people carrying precious rugs, caskets, and plants.

'Going in to sell them to the witches, I suppose!' whispered Hop. 'Look! The gates are opening! Get ready to slip inside!'

But just at that moment the mouse gave a shrill squeak.

The brownies looked round. They saw that the sack had fallen off the little mouse's back, and that hundreds of green labels were flying about all over the place.

'Oh! Oh! What shall I do?' squeaked the mouse. 'I shall be late, I know I shall!'

The brownies jumped up.

'Let us help you to pick them up!' said Hop. 'It won't take a minute.'

'We must hurry, though,' said Skip, 'or we

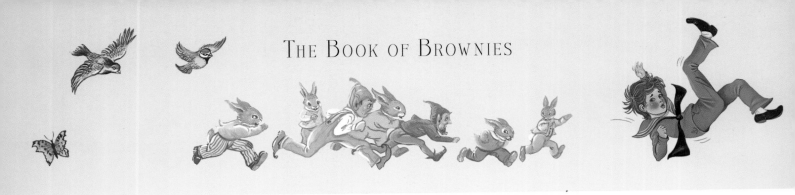

shan't get in whilst the gates are open.'

The brownies quickly picked up the labels and filled the mouse's sack again. He was very grateful indeed.

'Don't mention it,' said Hop, and turned to the gates of Witchland.

Clang! They shut, for the last of the procession had gone in!

'Oh my!' said Hop in dismay. 'Now we've lost our chance!'

The little mouse looked very upset. 'Did you want to get in?' he asked.

'Yes,' said Hop. 'But it doesn't matter – we'll wait till someone else wants to go in again, and the gates open.'

'I wish we could find something to eat,' sighed Skip. 'I'm getting so *dreadfully* hungry!'

'Won't you come home with me for a while?' asked the mouse. 'I'm sure my master, the Labeller, would give you something to eat, as you've been so kind in helping me.'

'Well, thank you very much,' said Hop. 'But what a funny name your master has – the Labeller! Whatever does he label?'

'Oh, whenever people are crosspatches, or spiteful, or horrid in any way,' said the mouse, 'they are taken to the Labeller, and he puts a label

round their neck that they can't get off. Then everyone knows what sort of person they are and, if they're very nasty, people avoid them as much as they can.'

'That seems a very good idea,' said Skip, as the brownies followed the mouse down a pathway. 'Do they have to wear the labels all their lives?'

'That depends,' said the mouse, trotting down a hole in a bank. 'You see, as soon as they stop being horrid, their label flies off, and goes back to the Labeller! If they go on being horrid for the rest of their lives, the label *never* flies off.'

'I say! The Labeller won't label *us*, will he?' asked Hop anxiously, as they all trotted down the hole after the mouse.

'Oh no!' said the mouse. '*You're* not horrid at all – you're very nice.'

The passage was lit with orange lights, and beneath every light was a little door. Each door had a name-plate on, and the brownies read them all as they passed by.

'Here's a funny one!' said Hop. 'The Bottler. I wonder what he bottles!'

'Oh, and here's the Labeller!' said Skip. 'The mouse is going inside.'

They followed him and found themselves in a cosy little room where a bright fire was burning.

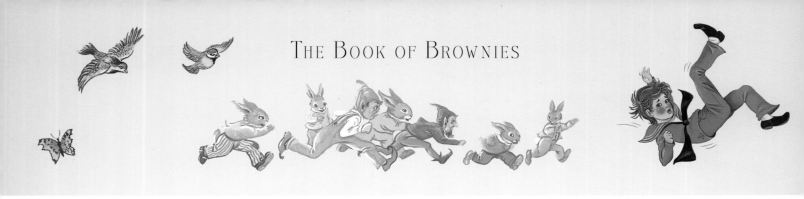

By a little table sat a fat old man with spectacles on. He was printing names on labels in very small and beautiful letters.

'Come in, all of you,' he said in a kind voice. 'I don't know who you are, but you're very welcome.'

The brownies said good-day politely and told him who they were.

'Where do you come from?' he asked.

'Brownie Town,' they answered.

'Well, what are you doing *here* then?' asked the Labeller in surprise.

The brownies went very red. Nobody spoke for a minute, and then Hop told the Labeller all about the naughty trick they had played at the King's party, and how the little Princess had been spirited away.

'Dear, dear, dear,' said the Labeller, 'that was a very silly thing to do. Perhaps I'd better label you all silly, had I?'

'No, thank you,' said the brownies quickly. 'We aren't silly any more. We're sorry for what we did, and we're trying to find the Princess and rescue her.'

The Labeller got out some buns and told the little mouse to make some hot milk.

'Sit down,' he said, 'and have something to eat. I'm sure it was very kind of you to help my little

servant to pick up all the labels he had dropped.'

The brownies each took and bun and said 'Thank you'.

'And when are you going back to Brownie Town?' asked the Labeller. 'When you've rescued the Princess?'

'No,' answered Hop sadly, 'we can't. The King said we weren't to go back until we had found our goodness – and people can't find their goodnesses, of course – so we're afraid we'll *never* be able to go back.'

'But of *course* you can find your goodness if you've got any!' said the Labeller. 'Why, my brother, the Bottler, can easily give you it if you've any that belongs to you. He bottles up all the goodness in the world, you know, and then, when anyone starts being peevish and grumpy, he seeks out his messenger – my mouse's cousin – to drop a little out of one of the bottles of goodness into something the peevish person is drinking. Then the grumpy person begins to smile again, and thinks the world is a fine place, after all.'

'Dear me!' said the brownies, in the greatest surprise. 'Is that really so?'

'And do you mean to say that if we've done any good deeds, for instance, the Bottler has got them boiled down and bottled up in a jar?' asked Skip in

excitement. 'Bottles that we can take away?'

'Oh yes,' said the Labeller, taking another bun. 'With your own names on and everything.'

'Well! If that isn't splendid!' cried Hop in delight. '*Could* we go and see if the Bottler's got any of our goodness bottled up?'

'Finish your milk and buns first,' said the Labeller, 'then you can go.'

The brownies finished their food and jumped up.

'Well, goodbye,' said the Labeller, shaking hands with them. 'The mouse will show you the right door. Good luck to you.'

Off went the brownies in a great state of excitement. They almost trod on the mouse's tail, they were in such a hurry.

They came to the little door marked 'The Bottler'. They knocked.

'Come in,' said a voice.

They went in, and saw a room like the Labeller's. It was full of thousands of bottles standing on hundreds of shelves.

The Bottler was very like the Labeller, except that he was a good deal fatter.

'What can I do for you?' he asked.

'Please,' said Hop in a shaky voice, 'please have you any goodness of ours bottled up?'

'Who are you?' asked the Bottler kindly.

'Hop, Skip and Jump, three brownies from Brownie Town!' answered Hop.

'Hm-m-m, let me see,' said the Bottler, putting a second pair of spectacles on. He walked up to a shelf labelled 'Brownies' and began peering at the bottles.

The brownies waited impatiently. Oh, if only, only, only a bottle of their goodness could be found, they could go back to Brownie Town.

'Ha! Here we are!' said the Bottler at last, pouncing on a little yellow bottle. It had something written on the label that was stuck round it. The Bottler read it out:

'"This goodness belongs to Hop, Skip, and Jump. It was made when they rescued a mermaid from the castle of the Red Goblin".'

'Oh fancy!' said Jump. 'I *am* glad we rescued Golden-hair!'

'Dear me, here's another bottle, too,' said the Bottler. He picked up a little green bottle and read out a label.

'"This goodness belongs to Hop, Skip, and Jump. It was made when they helped a little girl to escape from the Land of Clever People".'

'Buttons and buttercups!' said Hop. 'That's *two* bottles to take back.'

'And here's a third bottle!' said the Bottler suddenly, and picked up a red bottle.

'"This goodness belongs to Hop, Skip, and Jump. It was made when they rescued the Saucepan Man from the Golden Dwarf"!' read the Bottler.

'How perfectly lovely!' cried Jump. 'That's a bottle each! How glad I am that we *did* help those people when we had the chance.'

'Here you are,' said the Bottler, handing them the bottles. 'Take care of them, for they'll take you safely back to Brownie Town. Now goodbye. I'm glad to have been of some use to you!'

'Goodbye, and thank you very much,' called the brownies, and hurried out into the passage with their precious bottles. The little mouse was outside, waiting for them.

'If you like, I'll show you a secret way into Witchland,' he said. 'I'd be pleased to help you any way I could.'

Hop hugged the kind little mouse.

'Please show us,' he said. He put his bottle into his pocket and followed the mouse up the passage.

The mouse ran down passage after passage, and at last went up a very steep one.

'This leads into a witch's house,' he whispered. 'There's a big mouse-hole that comes out into the cellar. You can squeeze through it.'

'Thank you,' said Hop. 'Tell me, little mouse, what is the name of the witch who lives here?'

'Witch Green-eyes,' whispered the mouse.

'Witch Green-eyes!' said the brownies in surprise. 'Just the very witch we want!'

They said goodbye to the mouse, squeezed through the hole, and found themselves in a dark, smelly cellar.

'Well,' said Hop, 'now we'll soon see if we can rescue Princess Peronel!'